'I don't mess with married men.'

He laughed. 'Come on, angel. There were sparks flying between us and there was a chance we could have died down there. You practically begged me to show you what you'd been missing. Are you going to tell me that my being married would have made any difference?'

'I *am* telling you.'

'You would've died a virgin?' he mocked.

Charlotte looked him in the eye. 'And you would have died a married man.'

Dear Reader

Wouldn't it be wonderful to drop everything and jet off to Australia—the land of surf, sunshine, 'barbies' and, of course, the vast, untamed Outback? Mills & Boon contemporary romances offer you that very chance! Tender and exciting love stories by favourite Australian authors bring vividly to life the city, beach and bush, and introduce you to the most gorgeous heroes that Down Under has to offer…check out your local shops, or with our Readers' Service, for a trip of a lifetime!

The Editor

Ann Charlton wanted to be a commercial artist but became a secretary. She wanted to play piano but plays guitar instead, and she never planned to be a writer. From time to time she abseils, which surprises her because she is afraid of heights. Born in Sydney, Ann now lives in Brisbane. She would like to do more tapestry work and paint miniatures and has absolutely no plans to research a book in the Amazon or to learn to play the bouzouki.

Recent titles by the same author:

NO LAST SONG

LOVE
RULES

BY

ANN CHARLTON

MILLS & BOON LIMITED
ETON HOUSE   18-24 PARADISE ROAD
RICHMOND   SURREY   TW9 1SR

For Gladys and Edgar Flower, my parents.

First published in Great Britain 1992
by Mills & Boon Limited

© Ann Charlton 1992

Australian copyright 1992
Philippine copyright 1992
This edition 1992

ISBN 0 263 77572 0

Set in Times Roman 10 on 10½ pt.
01-9206-60480 C

Made and printed in Great Britain

CHAPTER ONE

THERE were schoolboys in the Champion House lift foyer, waiting for a glimpse of their hero and, maybe, an autograph. Even fallen heroes were better than none, Charlotte supposed. A large poster of Sam Buchanan in dynamic action, rocketing along the pitch, was displayed on the elevator wall. The caption read, 'Play it again, Sam'. Mrs Fulbright, a cricket supporter for over fifty years, looked impressed. Mrs Humphries, who wasn't interested in sport but was susceptible to the aura of the famous, fixed her gloves for the third time. Charlotte, who had been raised in the aura of the famous and thought cricket was boring, remained detached.

Of course, she had read about Buchanan. Who could avoid it? In the sports pages his terrible current form was contrasted with his past glories. In the financial pages his successful Champions chain of sports stores was regularly examined. In the social pages, squiring some photogenic female at a charity dinner, he was epitomised as a man-about-town. He had even made the front page once or twice when his racy lifestyle and volatile temper put him in conflict with photographers. He sounded a thoroughly unpleasant character but Charlotte, aware of how intrusive the media could be, felt a sneaking sympathy for him all the same.

'I wonder if he *was* drunk. And if he *did* hit that photographer,' Mrs Fulbright said wistfully, wanting to believe that cricketers were gentlemen the way they used to be. 'The Press do exaggerate any little item about celebrities, as I'm sure you know, Charlotte. Perhaps we should take Mr Buchanan as we find him and put that very unpleasant nightclub incident from our minds.'

'And the umpire incident, too,' Mrs Humphries said.

'*And* the nude-girl-in-the-hotel-room incident,' Charlotte murmured. Mrs Fulbright looked disapproving that she'd raked up this scandalous morsel and Charlotte added pacifyingly, 'Sure to be exaggerated. I'll bet she had *something* on.'

There was a moment's silence during which they contemplated the nature of the beast they were about to confront.

'If only I knew his star sign,' Mrs Humphries said, as if the fate of their petition might rest on this vital information.

The Champions offices were functional, tasteful and without ostentation apart from the hushed, expensive silence that only came with first-class carpeting and acoustic design. On one wall was a collection of photographs of the Champions founder. Buchanan, shaking hands with Prince Philip. Buchanan with media personalities, accepting a Sportsman of the Year award and so on. In every picture he looked exactly the same—the broad grin framed by the flashy Zapata moustache that was his trademark. Caricatures of the smile and moustache were silk-screened on to every price-tag, every poster in his chain of sports stores. A slightly out-of-date trademark. Buchanan hadn't smiled like that for ages, not for the Press cameras anyway.

'We have an appointment with Mr Buchanan,' Mrs Fulbright told the receptionist. 'We're members of the Heritage and History Society.'

The girl gave a fugitive smile and got up and opened a door just wide enough to insert her svelte figure, closing it again quickly as if they were thieves ready to pounce on the treasures within. While she was gone, Charlotte looked at yet more pictures of Buchanan, this time with some of the Champions Sports of the Month. Not, as the name might suggest, genuine sportsmen and women, but pretty models with great figures who posed with golf clubs and snow skis. One lucky Sport of the Month became Sport of the Year and went on to adorn the cover

of Champions' famous annual catalogue and to become
Miss December on the Champions calendar, both pub-
lications in the finest traditions of female exploitation.
Not, Charlotte had to admit, that the models themselves
looked disgruntled about being exploited. As for the man
himself, he looked the same in these pictures as in the
sporting ones. Same smile, framed by the ridiculous,
riveting moustache. The eyes were barely visible slits,
deep set beneath straight brows, giving him an odd se-
crecy. The original masked man. She was mulling over
this unbidden description when the receptionist came
back and told them that Mr Buchanan had been unexpectedly called away.

'But his assistant will see you. This way.'

'It's Mr Buchanan we must talk to,' Mrs Fulbright
said with the gentle insistence that had saved a number
of buildings and artefacts from destruction. 'Regarding
some property of historical value that he owns.'

But the girl was already leading the way and they followed. Charlotte brought up the rear and, on her way
past, touched the closed door. It was ajar and swung
open on a large office. It adjoined a small gym. Behind
a rowing machine was another door from which came
the muffled sounds of water. Had he been 'unexpectedly
called away' to the shower? Charlotte hesitated. They
could hardly confront Buchanan in his executive
bathroom, nor could they wait for him and catch him
out in a blatant lie. It wouldn't do much for future ne-
gotiations if they cornered the owner of Cranston in a
towel. Behind the huge steel and perspex desk, a swivel
chair rocked slightly as if its occupant had only just
walked away from it. Or run, she thought derisively.
Pulling the door to, she followed the others.

Buchanan's assistant, Grahame Norris, smiled and
agreed with everything they said. 'Petition. OK. No
problems, girls.' He took the petition from Charlotte,
glanced at it then dropped it on to a corner of his desk,

perilously close to the waste paper basket. Charlotte picked it up again.

'One hundred and forty-six people signed this, Mr Norris, asking Mr Buchanan to reconsider his plans to demolish Cranston.'

'Quite understand your concern. Heritage—history. Very important. Wonderful work you people do. But in this case——' He flashed his teeth and shrugged, indicating that the battle was lost. 'Sam asked me to make his apologies. A temporary girl arranged your appointment and unfortunately it wasn't brought to his attention until it was too late to contact you. He would never have allowed you to come all this way had he known, because naturally he doesn't intend talking to you about his property now or at any time.'

Mrs Fulbright and Mrs Humphries gave small, audible gasps at this hard fact delivered with tender solicitude and, before they recovered, Norris was among them, guiding, nudging them to the door like a sheepdog herding the ewes. A thick wad of autographed Sam Buchanan photos magically appeared in his hands.

'For your nephews, grandkids,' he said, dealing them out impartially. In a matter of moments they had been mustered into the lift lobby. Norris held out his hand for the petition but Charlotte held on to it.

'I think we'll deliver this personally, Mr Norris. Even with you as—watchdog——' She'd almost said 'sheepdog' '—there must be a way we can see Mr Buchanan.'

The man flashed a toothy smile. 'Watch him on television, love. It's the closest you'll get.'

But they came closer than that only minutes later. As they waited to cross the road outside the Champions building, a black BMW emerged from the Champions basement. The driver wore a tucked, formal shirt and wrestled one-handed with a black bow tie. His head was turned away but what was on view was very smooth, very suave. There was a damp look to his hair, as if he'd just been in the shower. It still held the comb tracks. As a gap opened in the traffic, the car leapt forward and Charlotte had a blurred glimpse of the famous Zapata moustache.

'Oh. Wasn't that——?' Mrs Humphries said.

'In the black car?' Mrs Fulbright shaded her eyes with her Sam Buchanan souvenir photos.

The schoolboys rushed out on to the pavement for a glimpse of their fallen hero. A Press photographer came running up the car ramp, followed by a man with a notebook. Charlotte half raised the petition. They all stood in a row, watching the black car zoom across two lanes.

'The one that got away,' Charlotte said.

'What day is it?' croaked Gale, staggering from her bed to prop herself in the doorway. She shielded her eyes from the sunlight. 'Must you have the radio on so loud?'

'Friday.' Charlotte grinned unsympathetically at her hungover cousin. The radio volume was moderate but she turned it down further. 'Friday the thirteenth,' she added in sepulchral tones.

Gale groped around for the coffee-mug Charlotte held out to her. 'Black Friday.'

'Black coffee.'

'Very funny.'

'I take it you had a wonderful time last night?'

Gale gave a groan. 'Fantastic. Can I borrow your overnight bag for the weekend, Charls? Say yes; I've already got some stuff packed in it.'

'You might ask me first when you borrow something,' Charlotte said. 'Are you sure you feel well enough to go away?'

'Of course. It'll be a brilliant weekend. We're going to watch horror videos all night tonight—you know, for Friday the thirteenth.'

'*All* the videos you watch are horrors,' Charlotte said, but her cousin had gone. She turned the volume up on the radio to hear two familiar voices singing a familiar song. Gale came back, partly dressed for work, and drank another cup of black coffee while Charlotte stowed a picnic lunch in her knapsack.

'That's one of their best,' she said of the song, gesturing at the radio. Charlotte agreed and opened the fridge, searching for the half-bottle of wine she was certain she'd put there, but the sole bottle of Riesling was a large one and belonged to Gale. It had a piece of paper impaled on its neck with 'GALE' written on it to remind her of the fact. She viewed it with irritation. Why was it that chronic borrowers were so often possessive about their own things?

'What's the picnic lunch for?' Gale asked.

'I've got the day off. Plan A was to have lunch with Martin and Linda but they had to cancel. So it has to be Plan B.' It was always wise to have a plan B where her parents were concerned. Plan As rarely eventuated. 'I'm going to photograph a house for the historical society. It's out near——'

'A day *off*,' Gale wailed. 'That's not fair. And you're going to spend it on one of your crumbling country mansions? You must be nuts rambling around on your own, haunting old houses. Aren't you scared you'll bump into a psychopath, or worse?'

'I saw some Boy Scouts once.' Charlotte didn't ask what was worse than a psychopath. 'This house is a bit different. It's been owned by descendants of the same family since it was built and you'll never guess who owns it now.'

But Gale glimpsed herself in the door of the microwave oven and gave a little scream. 'Look at my hair! *Hot rollers*!' she cried the way someone might call for water to put out a fire. She ran to the bathroom and anxiously applied mousse, hair thickener and gel to selected sections of hair while the rollers heated. Charlotte followed her in and leaned in the doorway, drinking her coffee and watching the feverish activity,

reflecting that Gale would have enjoyed hearing about
Buchanan, and his elegant offices and his crumbling
country mansion. But Gale, like other members of her
family, had a very short attention-span.

'If you spent as much time improving your mind as
you do your hair, you'd be a genius,' she commented.

Gale shot a critical look at Charlotte's straight, rather
limp fair hair. 'And if you spent some time on your hair
instead of pondering over poetry and taking snaps of
ruins, you'd look fantastic. You're a lot like Auntie
Linda, you know. I *wish* you'd let me crimp your hair
some time,' she said. 'It could change your life.'

'Why would I want to change my life?' She ignored
Gale's pained expression. 'Anyway, I don't fancy
crimped hair much.' Charlotte ran a hand uninterestedly
into her hair and glanced at herself in the mirror. Not
much like Linda at all, she felt. Even now, at forty-plus,
her mother was considered quite beautiful. Charlotte had
inherited her mother's high arched brows and full mouth
and her father's grey-blue eyes but somehow missed
being as striking as either of her parents. As she'd also
missed out on their flair for dramatising themselves, she
was a rather pale presence in their lives. Not the kind
of daughter expected of two recording stars. She couldn't
even sing. From the kitchen came the closing bars of the
familiar song. The familiar voices faded out. 'And that
was Earthbound——' the disc jockey said. Charlotte had
been hearing them like this for too long for it to be a
novelty but she always found it distracting. Her parents
really did have the most marvellous harmony.

'If I was suddenly given a Friday off,' Gale said, still
rankled by Charlotte's good fortune, 'I wouldn't waste
it taking pictures of some old ruin. I'd fly up to the Gold
Coast, sleep late, smoke *inside*.' She sent Charlotte a
dark look at this. 'Eat what I like, get a terrific tan, do
the casino and nightclubs until dawn——' She gave a
little burst of hairspray to mark each of these activities.

'And come home again flat-broke, with sunburn, heartburn and circles under your eyes. Your holidays are a health risk.'

'And you, of course, *never* put your health at risk.'

'Oh, I wouldn't say that,' Charlotte said mildly, dragging her hair to one side and idly surveying the result. 'Yesterday I nearly got beaten up by a drunken father.'

'Whose father?'

'Christopher Dunlop's. I told him Christopher had a good brain and he should consider letting him stay on to finish school. I also mentioned that his son ran into rather a lot of doors, especially on weekends. For a while I thought he was going to hit me, but I suppose even he couldn't bring himself to floor a teacher.'

'Don't know why you bother about that little Christopher creep after what he did to your car. He'll turn out a bully like his father whatever you do. It's in their genes.'

'Bullies are made, not born.'

'Have it your way. Speaking of genes—can I borrow your Levis for the weekend? My good ones aren't washed.'

'No, you can't. I want to wear them today.'

'Oh, be a sport. You've got a whole wardrobe full of clean stuff,' Gale wheedled, as if it were some unfair quirk of nature that Charlotte's clothes were usually washed and ironed and hers were not. 'I tell you what, I'll loan you my spare rabbit's foot for good luck if I can have your jeans,' she bartered. 'Remember it's black Friday. Thirteen's lucky for some but for others——' She dragged a finger across her throat and made a choking noise.

'A truly amazing offer, but no, thanks. I have no inclination to wear the amputated parts of some hapless animal.'

Gale went away grumbling that blood was supposed to be thicker than water and, after a serious session with nail polish and make-up, was ready to leave with the hijacked overnight bag stuffed full of crumpled clothes. 'See you Monday night, Charls. Keep away from black cats and don't walk under any ladders. You don't want to put your health at risk!'

After she'd gone Charlotte found that her cousin had taken the jeans after all. Angrily, she dressed in a pair of baggy walking shorts instead. Then she went to the fridge, removed Gale's note of ownership with a flourish and packed the bottle of wine in her bag.

She had taken the wrong track. The left, had she followed it, would have led her straight to Cranston, but her sense of direction wasn't great so she'd taken the right and now the house lay above her. Its chimneys were just visible over the highest rise. A crow circled lazily over them, black against a blue sky. Charlotte set down her knapsack and camera-bag and mopped her face. The sunlight was too strong for September, more like the blaze of midsummer, bleaching colour from the grass. Heat lay, thick as a quilt, in the landfolds that sloped up from the creek where she stood. The ground was rocky, the house seemed miles uphill and her boots had rubbed sore spots on her heels. Beguiled by images of cold running water, she picked up her bags and plunged into the bush that thicketed the creek.

The prince never would have made it to Sleeping Beauty through this, she thought as she fought a right of way with spindly rosebriars and spiky, dead thistles. Just when she had decided that cold running water wasn't worth the effort, she broke through to the creek. It was deeper here, bottle-green in the shade, silver where the sun flicked the surface. The water flowed, making trickling, gurgling sounds like half-formed words. Bees busied themselves in the gnarled flowering peach trees that overhung the creek. A dragonfly flitted across the water in nervous starts.

The fruit trees and the run-wild rosebushes suggested
this had once been planted as a garden, perhaps by some
early Hawker wife as a reminder of England and a refuge
from the harshness of the Australian summer. Charlotte
looked around for further evidence and saw letters carved
on a massive river gum. Graffiti, she thought, wrinkling
her nose. As if she didn't see enough of that in the school
grounds. But this was a superior graffito, the words borrowed from a master.

'Robert and Emma. Journeys end in lovers meeting.
We met by chance Wednesday 26th day of June. AD
1839.'

Charlotte ran her fingertips over the carving. There
was a note of thanksgiving about it, as if Robert and
Emma couldn't quite believe their luck. Had they taken
one look at each other and known? It was possible. How
else would they remember the exact date of their first
meeting?

She smiled wryly at her romantic fantasy. Who believed in love at first sight any more? Dropping her bags,
she took out her camera and tripod and set up for a shot
of the inscription.

Pink blossoms fell in the creek to float with the slow
motion current. White bubbles drifted downstream. Out
of sight a fish splashed in the water, sending ripples over
the surface to rock the bubbles and blossom. Charlotte
bent to look through the viewfinder, fitted a brown filter
to deal with the flash of sun on water, zoomed for the
shot—the tree-trunk with the creek behind it was re-
produced in miniature in the camera window. The ripples
raced in closer and closer together. Pink flowers bobbed
crazily and were inundated. If it was a fish, it was a big
one. Hand pushed through the side-strap, eye to the
preview window, Charlotte frowned and waited for the
surface to even out.

The water heaved. Charlotte gaped as a man appeared
in her picture. A big man, naked and shining, his body
coppery brown, his head a curious moulded silver.

Wading in the thigh-deep water, he reached out for
something, a floating bottle or container that spun in
the eddies around him, and tossed it ashore. Then he
dipped his head in the water and scrubbed at it. White
shampoo bubbles spread around him as he sluiced and
rinsed. Finally he straightened and threw back his head,
spraying water in a glittering arc. One big hand swept
back over his hair, squeezing runnels of excess water
down his neck and shoulders.

Arm upraised, hazed by sunlight, he looked heroic,
cast in bronze, a sculpted relic of ancient Rome raised
from the deep. A few pink flowers nudged at his muscular thighs like votive offerings to a woodland god. Or
a god of fertility. Charlotte stared into the camera
window, bemused by this idyllic yet erotic composition.
The man lifted his head suddenly, like an animal scenting
the wind. Hands on hips, he slowly turned, searching
the banks and still she didn't look up, convinced it was
an illusion that would vanish if she took her eyes from
the viewfinder. Her index finger rested on the shutter
button.

His start of surprise when he saw her, the hunching
of those big shoulders as he set hands on hips, was riveting, like watching a movie.

'I hope you got my good side,' he said baring big white
teeth. The travesty of a smile vanished in an instant.
Water surged around his thighs, bubbles and pink flowers
eddied and sank in his wake as he waded to the bank.
The sound of his voice brought her head up at last and
the miniature vision of male perfection magnified into
an unshaven, long-haired, glowering giant. Bits of grass
and dirt flecked his long, hairy legs. A scar above his
eye and another on his ribs brought images of street-
fights with broken bottles to mind. Only a chestful of
tattoos would make him look tougher, but she gulped
back hysterical laughter when she saw where one of the
pink blossoms clung perkily, like a gift decoration. She

had a strong urge to go back to the viewfinder and min-
iaturise him again.

'You've got a nerve, angel.' His ferocious advance
came to a stop as he stepped on something in the water
and let out a string of curses intended as much for her
as for the pain in his foot. 'You needn't think I'm letting
you leave here with—ow!' He hopped on one leg, examined the other.

Not let her leave? Charlotte glanced around, conscious of her isolation. 'Aren't you scared you'll bump
into a psychopath...?' It was ludicrous. But the man
was bad-tempered and scarred with former combat of
some kind and she didn't feel like waiting around for
him to regain the use of both legs. Shaking, she removed
her camera and looped it around her neck, hoisted her
bags over her shoulder and, toting the tripod like a lance,
ran.

'Hey!' he yelled.

Driven to Olympian efforts by the sounds of pursuit,
she trampled through the undergrowth and into what
was obviously his camp site. Panting, she dodged a red
tent and a motorbike, leapt a pile of empty beer cans,
a frying pan, an axe, a mallet, and a low bush spread
with drying underpants. Some itinerant, camping il-
legally, polluting the creek with soap and shampoo.
Labouring through the bushes, heart pounding,
Charlotte decided vengefully that she would report him
to the property agent.

'Wait a minute will you, you damned fool? Don't you
go wandering—ouch! Damn!'

The tangle of rosebriars and scrub was no place for
a naked man. He let loose with some heartfelt curses
and yelled something else too, urgently, but she had left
him behind and the words didn't carry.

Because the track she had come on would take her
back past the man's territory, she hared uphill towards
the house, dodging between trees and rocks for cover.
On high ground at last she stopped, heaving and sweating

in the sun, to look down at the creek. Nothing moved
in the thicket of trees, nor on the undulating slopes
around it. The man was probably tending his wounds
or drinking beer, or both.

She turned and saw Cranston for the first time. The
several engravings and early photographs she'd seen of
it didn't prepare her for its impact. Hazed in sunlight,
Cranston's stone was warmed to a pale apricot, the
architectural details fuzzed into soft focus. How could
Buchanan even think of demolishing a work of art like
this? The illusion of wholeness dissipated as her eyes
grew accustomed to the glare and the signs of aban-
donment came into sharp focus. The row of keystone
arched entrances, so pleasing in proportion, gaped
doorless; all the windows were broken. Bits of masonry
lay in the grass.

She longed to explore but didn't feel safe even this far
from that barbarian. At the thought of him, she moved
forward. From the topmost branch of a dead tree, the
crow called, 'Farquhar, Farquhar.' The buckles on
Charlotte's backpack jingled, the grass rustled past her
ankles. No other sound in the drugged silence. She was
almost within the shadow of the house when the motorbike snarled.

Heart pounding, she whirled and looked down at the
thicketed creek. The sun struck glints off the big black
machine as it charged from shadow on to the blonde
slope of grass and dandelion. Bike and rider dipped into
a hollow then appeared again to stop on a rise. There
was no mistaking the man's purpose. He stood and raised
a hand to his eyes, turned his head through a hundred
and eighty degrees. He was looking for her.

Charlotte tried to tell herself he was probably just joy-
riding. Going to the pub to buy some more beer. But
he'd looked foul-tempered, and she thought of all those
news bulletins reporting crimes against women. 'Fears
are held for the safety of a schoolteacher, missing
since...' When he disappeared into another landfold she

sprinted for the sanctuary of the old house. Inside one of the doorways, she pressed back against the wall and listened to the rise and fall of the bike engine. This, she thought with a wild attempt at humour, was like the plot of one of Gale's horror video movies. Girl pursued by naked, smiling psychopath takes refuge in deserted old house. Only, in Gale's favourite gory films, the psychopath usually wielded an axe. She swallowed. In her mind she reviewed in fine detail the things that had flashed past her as she ran through his campsite. A fishing knife half buried in the ground, the wicked glitter of sunlight along the blade of an axe. Her heart beat so violently that the bottle of wine and the vacuum flask in her backpack set up a rhythmic clink.

The bike came closer. Charlotte retreated inside, skirting around the roof slate that had fallen through, carrying with it part of the upper floor. Past a staircase that now led nowhere, she went, one part of her mind registering the irrelevance of the house's ruined beauty. Failing to find a hiding place, she backed into a large, stone-floored kitchen as the roar of the bike expanded and swelled to fill the house then, abruptly, stopped. Footsteps travelled along the stone terrace and inside the house.

'Hey, angel. Come out if you're there.'

Come out, come out, wherever you are. Like a child's game of hide-and-seek, she thought inanely. A psychopath would enjoy a game of hide-and-seek, cat-and-mouse. Footsteps came closer and she shrank into the only hiding place the kitchen offered, the dark at the top of the cellar steps.

'You with the boots—can you hear me?'

Boots? Charlotte looked down at her Army surplus boots. Inexplicably, she found this reference more frightening than anything. Her skin crawled. There was a long silence then he went outside again. *A psychopath—or worse*. What was worse than a psychopath? Charlotte waited in vain for the departing

sound of the motorbike. An intermittent thumping
began. What was he doing—vandalising the place? Ears
tuned to every permutation of sound, she gazed at a
sprouting of thistle that flourished in a patch of sun on
the kitchen floor. There was white dust, like talcum
powder, all over the prickly leaves. Vaguely she felt there
was some conclusion she should draw from the sun and
the dust.

'Ow! *Hell*!' he exclaimed, distantly enough to prompt
her to move. One step she took when her tripod, now
telescoped, knocked against the wine bottle in her pack.
The clink echoed down into the cellar.

He came into view suddenly, silhouetted in the patch
of sunlight that nourished the weed. His face was in-
distinct because of the shade but the light limned his
head and one ear, gilded the tangle of hairs on his fore-
arms. Over his shoulder he toted something by a handle.
Charlotte closed her eyes. Not an axe, surely not an axe.

'What the hell are you doing there?'

At least he had put on some clothes. She didn't know
why, but she felt absurdly grateful for that.

'Didn't you hear me calling you?' he demanded. He
beckoned, palm up, like a policeman directing traffic.
'Come on, come on. Out.'

It wasn't an axe, it was a mallet. Her relief was overwhelming but short-lived. Being bludgeoned to death was
only degrees better than being attacked with an axe. 'The
body of a woman was discovered by Boy Scouts in a
remote area...' Charlotte pulled herself together. When
he seized her arm and yanked her out into the thin beam
of sunlight, she lashed at him with the tripod.

'For Pete's sake!' he yelled, raising an arm against the
onslaught. There was talcum powder on his arm, she
noticed as she belted him yet again. It was incongruous
enough to distract her. He didn't look the talcum powder
type. She was dusted with the stuff as well. The same
stuff that covered the weed. It was in the air, floating.
That earlier worry firmed into a conclusion. Sun shining

on the middle of the kitchen floor meant a hole in the upper floor and roof. She looked up as a low groan came from above. It sounded like a tree, cut through and just beginning to fall.

Cursing, the man dropped the mallet, shoved her down one step and slammed her against the wall. 'My tripod——' she wailed, as she lost her grip. Something glanced off her head before his arms came up to shield her. A chunk of timber hurtled down and hit the spot where they'd stood a few seconds before.

Her face was squashed between his neck and the bunched muscle of his raised arm. Her nose was filled with a salty man-smell compounded of creek-water, shampoo and petrol fumes. She opened her mouth and found herself chewing on folds of warm T-shirt. Cold, unyielding stone behind her and warm, unyielding man in front. She shivered, more from the heat than the cold. The crushing pressure eased from her shoulder and thighs. Charlotte surfaced like a drowning swimmer and gulped air. Looking skyward, he transferred a handcuff grip to her wrist and said, 'Right. Let's go.'

'My tripod——' she said, feeling the loss of something to hit him with. He yanked her past it.

'Forget the blunt instrument,' he said drily.

In view of the fact that bits of roof were falling and that the man might well only be saving her for a worse fate, she probably should have forgotten the tripod. But Charlotte's thrifty soul was outraged and the tripod seemed suddenly terribly important. She leaned yearningly towards it but he swept her out into the flagged kitchen.

It was as if Cranston had been waiting until they ventured into the open. As they reached the patch of sunlight, an earthenware chimney-pot that had sat serenely on the roof for a hundred and fifty years sailed down to shatter on the stone floor. Its shrapnel drove them back again. From the top step they retreated downwards, then again as Cranston's roof beams shuddered

and trembled and sent roof slate and chimneys sliding
into the house along the increasing slope.

'Hell and damnation, the whole lot's going! We'll have
to wait until it stops now,' he yelled.

The roof spilled inwards, crashed on to the upper floor,
weakening the edges of the hole there and splintering the
floorboards directly over the steps. Further into the cellar
they reeled as the upper floor was ripped apart and debris
slammed down over the cellar steps. A massive beam
speared down, end-first, like a caber thrown by some
giant Scot, to lodge diagonally across the stairs. Others
jammed around it. The rumble grew to a roar, dust
swirled in the air and the cellar was plunged into
darkness.

At last the noise stopped. The pall slowly settled and
a thin ray of sunlight filtered through the rubble, lending
the cellar stairs a glum greyness. Charlotte and the man
stood motionless for a long time then they moved
forward together, their timing synchronised by shock and
disbelief.

A mighty crash vibrated the stone floor beneath them.
As they leapt back, the rubble on the steps jerked forward
and compacted as if some giant had rammed it into place
and slammed down the final piece of Cranston to hold
it there.

CHAPTER TWO

SILENCE then. All but the sibilant whisper of settling dust and miniature avalanches made by the shift of something larger. There was no sound at all for maybe five minutes.

Charlotte cleared her throat. 'Well,' she said, quelling the panic stirring deep inside her, 'this probably isn't as bad as it looks.'

He turned at her forced bright tone. She saw him in deep shades of grey through the murky light. Waves of dust and hostility engulfed her. 'And how bad does it look to you, angel?'

She gulped, coughed. 'We must be able to move some of that.'

'*We*?' The word ground out between clenched teeth. 'You mean *me*, don't you? You mean, now that you've got us into this mess, I should act like Superman and get us out.'

'What do you mean, *I've* got us into this?'

He spun away from her, picked up chunks of brick and slate from the steps and flung them to the far wall, more to vent his temper than for any useful purpose. Charlotte flinched at each impact.

'What is it with women?' he snarled. 'Three weeks I've camped by the creek. For three weeks I've had peace and solitude and nothing but snakes and the mosquitoes to bother me, then a *woman* turns up and within one bloody hour the roof falls in on me!' He seized a length of splintered timber and pointed it at her. 'This is all your fault. If you hadn't hung back for that bloody tripod, we'd have got out just in time.'

'I paid a lot for that tripod,' she said weakly in self-defence. 'It's ultra-light and has automatic——'

'I don't give a damn if the bloody thing doubles as a periscope!' he roared. 'You come wandering around, no thought for your own safety—trespassing.' He seized on the word, flung it at her again with as much weight as if it was 'murder'. '*Trespassing*!'

'I wasn't trespassing. Naturally I sought permission before I——'

'You *sought* permission,' he mocked. 'I don't recall giving you permission to come nosing around my property.'

'You?' She shook her head. 'This property is owned by Sam Buchanan and——' Her voice dried up. Hadn't she seen that pose of his, mallet over his shoulder somewhere before? On an office wall. Replace the mallet with a cricket bat...the face was all wrong, and yet... 'You're Sam Buchanan?' she said, in a cracked voice.

'Oh, come on. Don't give me the innocent act. You know who I am—otherwise why were you furiously taking pictures of me in the buff? What I want to know is, how the hell did you track me down? Which gossipy little tabloid do you work for?'

She gave a short laugh that was equal parts shock, confusion and suspended panic. 'No—I don't work for a newspaper and I wasn't trying to track you down. Well, not today anyway——'

'What?'

'We missed you at your office,' she babbled, relieved that he wasn't a psychopath or worse but unexpectedly unnerved by Sam Buchanan in the flesh. 'We could have waited, I suppose. Had we been militant, we would have stormed your office and no doubt found you in your executive shower.'

He was looking at her now as if it was she who was unhinged.

'Had we been militant?' he repeated. Suspicion narrowed his eyes. 'We?'

'Myself,' she said, 'Mrs Fulbright and Mrs Humphries—from the Heritage and History Society. We came last month with a petition.'

He looked positively murderous. 'You mean you're one of those interfering old biddies——' A raked glance over her bare young legs appeared to remind him that she didn't fit the description. Grahame Norris's description, no doubt.

'Two old biddies, one young biddy,' she said coldly.

'—one of those interfering, sanctimonious *busybodies*,' he amended, 'who want to have this *dump* listed with the National Trust?'

'Only as a last resort, to save it. It's all in our letters. You obviously haven't had time to answer them yet,' she said with the barest trace of irony.

His head thrust forward. 'Here's my answer, angel. Stay out of my affairs. I don't intend to have my property tied up for years while a bunch of do-gooders and bureaucrats decide what I can and can't do with it. And if I catch any of you trespassing on my property again, I'll prosecute.'

'I wasn't trespassing. The property agent gave me permission to——'

'The property agent just lost himself a client. He obviously hasn't been out to check the place or he would have put up a warning sign. There's a hole in the roof and bits have been falling all week. I *sought* to warn you back there,' he said, heavily sarcastic, 'but you took off like a scalded cat.'

'Oh. Is that why you were coming after me on the bike, to warn me about the roof?'

'Why did you think I was coming after you, angel?' he said with a music-hall leer.

'How would I know? A—a——' Naked sounded too earthy. Nude too provocative. 'An unclothed man——'

'Unclothed?' he snorted.

'—looking like an all-in wrestler, scarred and swearing and clenching his fists and threatening to detain me——'

'*Detain*? It wasn't you I couldn't part with, angel. But I wasn't going to let you get away with all those pictures of me and my rubber duckie.' His eyes strayed to the camera still hanging around her neck and she gathered her bags protectively close around it.

'I didn't know that! You could have been a psychopath or worse, as far as I knew. Wouldn't you run, if you were a woman in those circumstances?'

The question clearly threw him. Buchanan's eyes glazed over with the effort of imagining himself a woman. 'What's worse than a psychopath?' he muttered, then, balefully still trying to pin the blame on her, 'You should have recognised me. You should have *guessed* who I was.'

'If you hadn't have shaved off the moustache, I might have. The only time I've ever seen you in the——' flesh, she almost said, inappropriate considering the way she'd seen him the *second* time '—in person, you were in your glossy car on your way to some celebrity gala. Your hair was all slicked back, you were fixing a bow-tie and hiding behind that ridiculous moustache. It didn't occur to me that a scruffy, unshaven itinerant, bathing in the creek, was the man-about-town Sam Buchanan, mostly found bowling people over in bars and nightclubs!'

Involuntarily, he traced the shape of the extinct moustache in a pincer movement of finger and thumb before he caught back the motion. The look he gave her was pure dislike.

'So what was the camera for? Are you here spying for your action group? Going to get some shots of irreplaceable historical features to get me snarled up in red tape.'

'Going to get some shots of an irreplaceable building before it vanishes,' she amended. 'Partly for the Society's historical files, but it's my hobby too.' She felt odd, light-headed, and hugged her bags to her as if she were a child and they her favourite teddy-bear. So far her voice remained steady, but shock was making her tremble deep inside. 'I take pictures of old houses before they fall apart or are knocked down. I'm going to write a book about it one of these days,' she said, her voice pitched unnaturally high. 'I might call it *Haunting Old Houses*, because that's what my cousin says I do—I'm always haunting old houses, you see the pun?' Dust tickled her throat and made her cough and the cough turned into unsteady laughter. 'I never do anything to put my health at risk! Gale said that only this morning.' Her laughter grew louder.

'Stop that,' he growled, giving her arm a shake. But she couldn't stop laughing and she couldn't stop talking.

'Oh, wait till Gale finds out...she'll die laughing. Don't walk under ladders, she said, because it's Friday the thirteenth today. Did you know that? Today is black Friday. Some people think thirteen is unlucky for them and others think it's their lucky number. I've never found out which it is for me. What do you think? Is thirteen *my* lucky number?' She laughed so much, she lost her balance and took a few small staggering steps to recover. 'Oh, *I* know what I did wrong today! I should have taken the rabbit's foot she offered me!' She threw back her head and her shrieks hit a high note.

He held her with both hands and shook her and when that didn't work, slapped her. Sharp and efficient, it stopped the hysteria dead. Astounded, she cradled her stinging cheek.

'You didn't have to hit so hard,' she said, glaring.

'Blame it on the poor light.'

'Oh, does it affect you that way? Like a full moon?'

'I might have misjudged,' he said unsentimentally. 'But things are tough enough. A hysterical woman I don't need. Calm yourself and come and help me shift this beam.'

Shaken by her brief loss of control and by his even briefer response, she put down her bags, stowed her camera carefully and did as he said. The beam wouldn't budge.

'It must weigh a ton,' he panted.

'Ironbark,' she said, straining every muscle. 'The timber for this house was probably cut on the property or nearby and hauled by ox cart. It would have taken five or six men to handle that beam into place. Henry Hawker—let me see—he would have been your maternal great-great-great grandfather—must have had some of the last convict labour to be assigned in New South Wales to help with the building. Labour was very short when the gold rush started around 1840——'

'Quit the historical notes, will you? We'll try levering it. Stay back.' Cautiously he stepped around the rubble on the lower steps, removing some lengths of floorboard which he wedged under the beam. It shifted a fraction and the unstable mass rumbled as chunks of brick and stone shifted to fill the gaps. He peered up the stairs then retreated gingerly. 'Move away and don't touch anything,' he told her. 'There's another beam lodged halfway down and ready to roll. If we move anything, the whole lot will come down like an avalanche.'

Charlotte saw what he meant. The steps were stoutly built of stone, encased each side in a stone wall—a steep, thin corridor laced with debris. The beam in question was balanced on broken chimney brick and roof slate. Its end was jagged, splintered and pointed downwards. In the walled staircase it looked like some cruel medieval trap waiting to be sprung. Unless they found a way to spring it by remote control, they ran the risk of being crushed without any guarantee that they could force an exit through the rubble above.

Buchanan peered around. The murky light didn't reach into the corners. 'Maybe there's another way out.'

'Don't you know?' she said, amazed that anyone who owned a house like this didn't know every little detail.

'No, I do not.'

'But the house has been in your family for a century and a half.'

'I haven't been around that long,' he said sardonically. 'My mother's family isn't on good terms. This house is as much a mystery to me as my Uncle Ralph's reason for leaving it to me.'

'Oh. Well, it was once considered the finest mansion around. Governors used to dine here and your forbears used to host grand occasions in the ballroom. Henry Hawker's wine cellar was the envy of early settlers in Sydney and Parramatta. He started a vineyard and made good wine until the vines were blighted with phylloxera——'

He rolled his eyes. 'Look, can we postpone the Michelin guide to past glories? I want to get out of here. Tell me something useful.'

'Sorry,' she said stiffly. 'I always talk too much when I'm nervous. There might be another entrance from the driveway for delivery of wine barrels, sides of beef, things like that—I've got a torch,' she said, crouching down to take it from her knapsack pocket. Her hands were still shaking.

'Now that's the first useful thing you've said.' The tiny pencil torch was plucked from her hand. He switched it on and played it around and she saw some timber fruit crates which held an assortment of junk and some old newspapers—a basin half filled with opaque water and beside it a cracked sliver of soap. A grey blanket lay alongside a chipped bowl containing beads and bits of copper and tangled cord. There was a dilapidated stretcher and under it a chipped enamel chamberpot, mercifully empty.

'Squatters,' said Buchanan, shining the torch on a gallery of tattered posters stuck to the wall. 'They've been coming here for a long time.' Graffiti was scrawled around the margins of the posters and overflowed on to the walls. 'Stamp out quicksand' and 'My wife's run away with my best friend. Gee, I miss him'. It was the usual mix of wit and foul language, the usual awful spelling that grated on her nerves. Buchanan glanced at her and flashed the torch past much cruder inscriptions. It was, she supposed, some vague gentlemanly impulse.

'It's all right. I've seen it all before. I'm a high school teacher,' she said wryly.

'A teacher. And me without an apple. What do you teach—history?'

'History is a hobby. I teach English and drama and sometimes Maths One.' An unenthusiastic grunt greeted this. 'You didn't like maths, Mr Buchanan?'

'Didn't like teachers.' His tone and his look informed her that he hadn't changed his mind since schooldays.

She shrugged and concentrated on finding an exit. There were air vents but they were cut into stone blocks at ground level, high above their heads and wide enough to take an arm, no more. They found the second entrance, filled in by less craftsmanlike stonework than the original, but every bit as solid. Buchanan strode around, ripping away rotting wine racks to get at the wall, sweeping aside the detritus of fifty years or more that had accumulated since the house was last lived in. Parts of old gas stoves, a length of drainage pipe, the round lid of an old copper that rolled across the floor and settled tinnily like an outsized tossed coin.

Buchanan turned his attention to the blocked staircase again where the light filtered through a gap in the rubble. Charlotte fancied she caught a glimpse of blue sky. It was unlikely, she realised, wishful thinking.

'Grab that crate and bring it over here,' he said, hauling the other one into position. He put the second crate on top of the first and stood on it, peering this way and that at the blockage. 'Hmm,' he said. 'Maybe I could—mmm. Perhaps if there was some—not too wide. Hmm—no rope——'

'Have you got an idea?' she asked. But all she got was another long silence then more 'hmms'. He got down and examined the staircase walls at close quarters, still muttering half-expressed ideas and discarding them without once sharing them with her.

'See if there's any old rope lying about,' he said.

He went off with the torch and she followed, left in the dark whenever he diverted into some nook or cranny. Charlotte, accustomed to taking charge, found his assumption of command irritating. Belatedly she remembered her portable lamp and stumbled to her camera-bag. The studio lamp, which she occasionally used to light an indoor shot on these excursions, flooded the cellar with light. The pop stars smiled and snarled from the walls.

'Great!' Buchanan said, moving in quickly to commandeer this new piece of equipment.

'Is there some unspoken law that says *you* must have the biggest light?' she said bitterly, losing the fight for it.

'Law of the jungle. I'm bigger than you,' he said, and slapped the tiny pencil torch into her palm.

'Look,' she said, trotting after him, 'I'm pretty tired of tripping along behind while you cogitate and bark out orders.'

'Cogitate?' He mimicked her precise diction. Then, as if the word had reminded him she was a teacher, said, 'How come you're wandering around here on a schoolday?'

'A politician visited the school last week and awarded us a special holiday.'

Buchanan muttered a few choice words about politicians. By this time it was chillingly obvious that there was no alternative way out. Frustrated, he slapped his hand against a stone block, almost as if he hoped to find it loose in its mortar. The light picked up the gleam of gold.

'You're married?' Even as she said it she recalled vague newspaper references to a marriage break-up, or was it

a divorce? She had never taken much notice of his publicity until she found out he was the owner of Cranston.

He snorted. 'Trust a woman to ask that at a time like
this. If Stanley had been a woman he wouldn't have said,
"Dr Livingstone, I presume", he would have said, "Are
you married?"'

'I couldn't care less about your marital status,'
Charlotte said coldly. 'But I wondered—hoped, there
might be a wife staying in that tent with you. In which
case we could reasonably expect her to come looking for
you.'

'No wife to come looking for me,' he said on a bitter
note. 'The ring is out of date but it won't budge. Have
to get a jeweller to cut it off for me one of these days.'

So it had been divorce. Charlotte felt bitter about it
herself. A wife would have been very convenient to raise
the alarm. Gingerly, she raked her foot into a dark corner
and uncovered an ancient cardboard carton which fell
to pieces at her touch. When she turned around,
Buchanan was a metre off the floor, his body bridging
the width of the staircase, feet planted on one wall, his
back pressed hard against the other. He straightened his
legs and pushed up a bit higher. Charlotte saw his plan
at last. If he couldn't get past the delicately balanced
beam, he would go over it. It was the way mountain
climbers went up narrow clefts and canyons—a technique for the superfit.

He stopped, grimacing and flexed his back. 'Is this a
good idea?' she asked, anxiously. 'It's a long way to the
top. If you fall you could be crushed under all that
rubble.'

He wasn't listening and he didn't seem apprehensive.
In fact there was a curious light in his eyes, almost as
if he was enjoying the challenge. She found it alarming.
Visions of herself trying to drag him out from under
that beam plagued her. What if she was stuck here overnight with a wounded man? 'I hope you're not going to
be all gung-ho and rush the ramparts, like a movie hero,'

she said sharply. 'If you have some repressed male fantasies about being Indiana Jones, don't play them out here. I don't want to be left holding the pieces.'

He looked down at her and bared his teeth a little. 'Be nice to me, angel. That way I might come back for you when I get out of here.'

'Don't call me angel. It's hard enough for women to be taken seriously without being lumbered with silly names more suitable for a rag doll.'

'What?'

'It's all right for you,' she said, nerves making her talk too much again. 'You're male and over six feet, which means you're taken seriously on sight. You should try being female and five feet five.'

He looked down with that glazed expression again. She wondered which was the more difficult—imagining himself female or diminutive.

'Anyway, my name is Charlotte Wells.'

'Angel, this is no time for introductions. I'm halfway up a wall without a safety net.' As he spoke he braced his feet and, jamming his body hard against the stone, pushed upwards. The muscular pressure required to keep him there, suspended across the passageway, was enormous. His thigh muscles were sharply defined and the effort put a shine on his skin, corded the sinews of his neck. Little by little, he made progress. Beneath him lay the unsprung trap. Charlotte clenched her hands and watched with the kind of helplessness that made her understand the old-fashioned phrase, 'women must wait'. A little further he went, and further still towards the light of day.

If anyone could do it, it was Buchanan. He was an arrogant, bad-tempered brute but fit and athletic. A good thing she hadn't got stuck down here with someone like Brian. It was a thought so disloyal, so crude that she was startled. She had never rated muscles and derring-do very highly in a man. Intelligence and sensitivity and a whole lot of other related factors seemed more important to Charlotte than a big chest and machismo. It was back to the cave, she thought, paying homage to Buchanan's streamlined body. When it came to survival what was needed was exactly those male characteristics she found dispensable in the safety of civilisation.

'You're almost there,' she called, as enthusiastic now as any of his fans as escape came closer. 'Sam, you're marvellous, you're almost there——'

His foot slipped. At first it seemed he had corrected in time, but in agonising slow motion Sam lost his leverage against the wall and slid sideways. 'Get out of the way!' he yelled, as he toppled, shoulder-first, into the debris. His head narrowly missed the splintered end of the beam, which gave an ominous shudder with his passing, and Sam Buchanan came down in a cloud of dust with bits of brick and stone bouncing around him. He catapulted into the cellar and went down like a felled ox. There was a pained 'Ooof' from him at the moment of impact, then nothing.

'Oh, no.' She crouched beside him, coughing in the dust fog. 'You can't be injured.' His stillness alarmed her. 'You just *can't*,' she croaked, bending to feel for a pulse and collapsing over him for a moment in relief when she found one. 'Alive. Thank God.' Shakily she examined his head, running her fingers into his damp hair. His skull was comfortingly undented and hard as a rock. 'Check for broken bones,' she muttered, recalling bits and pieces of the first-aid manual in the Staff Room. 'If you've broken something I'll have to set it while you're unconscious, otherwise——' Breathlessly, she pulled his shirt free and felt around his ribs. There were some small cuts and swellings. 'I've never set a broken bone. What did the manual say? Splints, I know you need splints and something to bind them with—have to tear up my shirt. Bandages in the first aid kit but I left that in the car,' she said, snivelling a bit. A few tears dropped on to Buchanan and she brushed them off. 'I only brought the sunscreen and some Band-aids.' She checked down his arms. The streamlined body she had admired just minutes before lay as helpless as a robot without a power supply, and she felt an overwhelming sadness, even a tenderness for him. It made her furious. 'Damn you! I told you not to play at being Indiana Jones.' She checked his ankles and patted up his legs. 'What am I supposed to do in a cellar with an unconscious man and no first-aid kit? How am I going to get out of here without you?'

'Nothing like a little womanly concern,' he said, opening his eyes and taking hold of her hands which were crawling around his thighs.

She all but collapsed on his chest in gratitude. 'You're all right! Thank God. Is there anything I can do?'

'Kiss of life?' he suggested. 'Or didn't the manual cover that?'

So he'd been conscious all the time, had he, while she'd raved and shed tears over him? She looked down at him, her heart pounding from shock, any vestige of tenderness gone now that those cynical eyes were open. He was hard as nails, alive and kicking and unlikeable. Now she was faintly disgusted with herself for admiring his physique even in the interests of survival. Flushing, she said drily, 'Don't joke about the kiss of life. Next time you might need it.'

'We all need the kiss of life from time to time, angel, to revive us when the going gets rough.'

'In your case, Mr Buchanan, wouldn't an iron lung be more efficient?'

His chest heaved in acknowledgement of the hit. 'Call me Sam,' he said. 'Or love, or darling, or sweetheart, I don't mind.'

'Sam,' she said firmly. She stood and when he raised a hand she took it and pulled in the spirit of co-operation. Groaning, Sam came up to a sitting position, then, in stages, to his feet. He grimaced and clutched at his left thigh but said it was nothing, an old muscle injury that played up from time to time.

'Tell me honestly—do you think we can get out of here ourselves?' Charlotte said.

'Only if we find a way to get past that rubble without being squashed. We might have to wait to be rescued.'

'How long do you think it will be before someone comes?'

'That depends on you.'

She dwelled on the statement with growing uneasiness. 'Why does it depend on me?'

'Because I went to a great deal of trouble to make sure that nobody knows where I am. How soon will you be missed?'

Charlotte thought about it a long time. 'Monday night,' she said at last, reluctantly.

'Monday—*night*?' He spaced the words out. 'Today is *Friday*!'

Dead silence. Charlotte did the sums. Friday to Monday was three days whichever way you looked at it. Three days, three nights. Sam stood up, and a cockroach went scuttling for cover.

'Why me?' he asked the posters on the wall. 'Why *me*? Did I let a black cat cross my path—did I open an umbrella indoors?' His foot came down with a thump and the sound of the cockroach stopped. Charlotte winced.

'The thing is,' she said, 'Monday night is when my cousin will miss me, but she won't know where to look. In fact,' she added soberly, 'I don't think anyone will know where to look.'

Another silence, longer this time. Then he gave a snort of disbelief. 'You must have told someone.'

Miserably Charlotte shook her head. 'I didn't decide to come here until last night so I haven't had a chance to tell anyone except Gale and she didn't listen——'

'The property agent,' Sam said. 'He'll know you're here.'

'I asked for permission weeks ago—he said I could come any time until Christmas or such time as the house was knocked down, whichever came first. So he wouldn't know and I don't think anyone would think to ask him, anyway.'

'The old biddies—your historical mates——'

'Mrs Fulbright and Mrs Humphries. They've gone touring in New Zealand with Mrs Fulbright's daughter. They'll be away for a month.'

'Well, *someone* in your historical group must know you were going to take photographs of this place,' he said irritably.

'I have a list of places to photograph for the society records. This is only one of them. Damn it! Why didn't I stay home today and wash the curtains?' she lamented. 'I could have gone to that seminar on Natural Health with Brian——'

'Who's he? Boyfriend?'

'A fellow teacher,' she said. 'We've been out a few times.'

'Didn't your fellow teacher want to know what you would be doing instead of going to lectures on bean sprouts with him?'

'I only told him Plan A,' she said, biting her lip.

He looked at her cautiously. 'Plan A,' he repeated without intonation.

'Plan A was lunch with my parents. They cancelled, so I came here instead. Plan B.'

'Did you tell your parents about Plan B?'

'No.'

'Why the hell not?'

'Look—they didn't have time for Plan A so they certainly didn't have time to listen to Plan B.'

He let out his breath in a ragged sigh. 'You must have let something slip somewhere. Neighbours, fellow teachers—er—the place where you bought your film. Amateur photographers are the gabbiest people on earth, always boring on about what shots they take and where——'

She shook her head to each of these.

'Your car!' He pointed at her. 'You've parked your car on the road—someone will see it there overnight and make enquiries.'

'I parked it under a willow tree—the branches come right down to the ground.'

'Why the hell did you do that?' he yelled, as if only the world's idiots parked under trees.

'For the shade. The sun isn't good for the duco——'

'I don't believe it! I have to get stuck with the only woman I've ever known to give a damn about her paint job!' Sam stuck his hands on his hips and glared. 'Do you do this often? Disappear into the countryside without leaving a trace, without telling anyone?'

'Do you?' she snapped.

He gave a grunt and turned away. Disconsolately, Charlotte walked around, shining the torch over the walls, unable to believe there wasn't *something* they had missed. 'Does the name Pavlov ring a bell?' some wit had written, and 'Graffiti is squatters' writes'. 'The squatters!' she exclaimed, excitedly flashing light over the stretcher, the basin of water, the soap. 'They live here!'

He gave a mirthless laugh. 'Not any more. I told them to move on two days ago.'

'But they might come back for—for—their blanket!' she cried, holding up the limp pile of grey fabric as if it was a prize no one would willingly relinquish. But it was threadbare and torn. Even the homeless wouldn't double back for it.

'They won't come back. I said if they did, I'd tell the police.'

'They were doing no harm,' she cried, full of spurious concern for the squatters who would not now conveniently return to help them. 'Why couldn't you have let them stay here?'

'Because I didn't want them to be *dead* squatters.' He strode around much as Charlotte was doing, looking for an exit they hadn't noticed, kicking at the walls and muttering dire threats to politicians, property agents and amateur photographers. 'I should have put up the warning signs sooner,' he said, accepting some of the blame himself at last.

'Signs.' Charlotte stared, remembering the mallet. 'That noise I heard—those vibrations, just before you came inside. Was that you, putting up signs?'

He frowned, nodded. 'Hell,' he said, looking at the ceiling. 'Vibrations—surely that wouldn't have been enough to set it off——' His voice trailed away without conviction.

'What did the signs say?'

'STAY OUT. ROOF MAY FALL.'

She was frightened half to death but she couldn't help seeing the humour in it. Sheer black comedy. 'You were hammering away at warning signs to protect stray visitors from a roof collapse and the roof might have collapsed because you were hammering away at the signs which were to protect——' Her laughter bubbled out and grew and in a few moments his laughter joined hers. And after they stopped laughing they both looked carefully again for a stray window or door or a hole in the ceiling. No exit.

'I hope you don't snore, angel,' Sam said.

'What?'

'Because it looks as if we're here for the night, and there's only one bed.'

CHAPTER THREE

CHARLOTTE studied the camp bed. It was disreputable in every way—the legs were shaky, the canvas dirty, but above all it was narrow. A furtive comparison between it and Buchanan convinced her that only the most intimate cramming would make room for her on the bed with that splendid body. And the alternative was a cold stone floor across which cockroaches scuttled. It was just one damned thing after another, she thought, feeling shaky again. Hastily she turned away as he noticed her preoccupation with the bed.

'Why don't we have some tea?' she said in a high, bright voice.

'Tea?' He looked narrowly at her, torn between hope of sustenance and suspicion that she was on the verge of hysterics again.

Charlotte rummaged in her backpack, glad to have something to do. At the sight of her picnic lunch packed so casually that morning, her stomach churned. She dusted off the top of a fruit crate with a tissue and spread a checkered napkin on it and set out the food. This picnic lunch should have been consumed hours ago, in the shade of a tree with flies buzzing and ants soldiering with leftover crumbs and a blue sky above. Charlotte felt panic drawing her down like quicksand. 'Sandwiches, fruit, cake.' She set each item of food out neatly on the napkin. 'Wine—it's sheer luck that I brought a large bottle of wine.' Sheer luck. The irony of the phrase made her laugh. 'I wouldn't have, except that Gale took my jeans.' She saw the glazed expression in his eyes. 'It was *her* bottle of wine,' she said in clarification.

'Ah, that explains it,' he said cautiously.

'A flask of tea,' she went on, finding some comfort in the inventory. 'And milk. I hope you don't take sugar because I haven't brought any.'

'No lemon?' he said drily, hunkering down to look into her backpack as if he expected to find it bottomless. He unscrewed the cap from the vacuum flask, Charlotte set out a plastic tumbler and he poured tea into both containers. They shared one small cheese and pickle sandwich. 'Better not eat everything at once,' he said. 'Just in case.'

The presence of food and drink had a cheering effect that carried them through to an assessment of their stores. Sam tasted the bottled water left by the squatters.

'Seems fresh enough. Collected from the creek, I suppose.'

'Upstream from where you wash your hair, I hope.' She met his scowl with a bland look.

He removed the chamber-pot and the basin with its few inches of washing water into the wine storage nook where there was some degree of privacy. Charlotte put the cracked piece of soap beside the basin and fetched a tiny hand towel from her backpack. Sam Buchanan regarded these refinements with ironic amusement. 'Let's play house,' he said.

Then there was nothing more they could do and time dragged. The therapy of action had given Charlotte a false feeling of control over her circumstances. As it vanished, her spirits sank again.

'Do you realise,' she said, breaking the long, depressing silence, 'that it is not beyond possibility that we might *never* be found?'

She stared in front of her, confronting the idea. It was almost dark now. The bunk was against the poster wall and they sat on it with a space for another person in between, like people in a doctor's waiting-room. As her statement sank in she said, in astonishment, 'Technically, we could die here. Oh, that's stupid! People can't die because they go out for the day to take some photographs and have a picnic lunch, can they?'

'Relax. We've got an air supply, food and water. We're a long way from dead.'

'I'm always telling my students that there's something positive in every adversity, if you only look for it,' she said gloomily.

'Keep looking, angel. Just don't go hysterical on me again.'

She didn't go hysterical on him. An hour passed in silence as they sat there on the bed, leaning back against the wall growing colder. She took her cardigan from her knapsack and put it on and still she was cold. Charlotte thought about her life and this situation and what might come of it and she didn't get hysterical, she got angry. She snatched the torch up and shot from the bed.

'It's not *fair*,' she yelled, flashing the light over the dingy interior and the scribbled walls. 'I've tried so hard. I've studied and I've worked long hours because I believe in what I'm doing and I've saved up until I've almost got enough money for a deposit on my own house—it's not *fair*! I haven't even started living yet! I've been getting ready to do all the things I wanted— I've been waiting. I've been——'

'Good?' he said sardonically.

'It's not funny!' she snapped. 'One of these days I thought I would travel, one of these days I would write my book! One of these days I was going to meet a man who was different from all the rest. I was waiting for the right one before I . . . oh, wouldn't that be priceless, if I'd waited for nothing? It wouldn't be *fair*!'

He laughed. 'Oh, angel. Haven't you heard? Life isn't fair. Simmer down. We might find a way to trigger off an avalanche on the steps without being buried—your cousin might remember the name of this place and send out a search party. An earthquake might drive your old biddies home from New Zealand early. We could be out of here Monday night. And if no one comes by Tuesday,'

he drawled, 'then I'll just have to play out my Indiana
Jones fantasies and rush the battlements come what may.'

'Monday night. Oh, *damn*!' Charlotte said, all self-
pity vanishing. She swiped the wall fiercely enough to
graze her knuckles. 'If I don't show up on Monday, I'll
lose Christopher.'

'I thought the boyfriend's name was Brian.'

'Christopher's one of my kids at school,' she said.
'Christopher Dunlop.'

'Teacher's pet?'

'Nobody's pet. He's insolent and pig-headed and dis-
rupts every class and never stirs himself to make an effort
for anything but playing the fool. He's a rotten, lying
little vandal!' She stopped for breath, hit the wall again.
'It's taken me a year to make him tell me what he wants.
A *year*!'

A small silence. When Buchanan spoke there was a
curious note in his voice. 'So what does Christopher
want?'

'To build things,' she said. 'He wants to build things
and he thinks he's too dumb and the system is against
him and his father's beaten all the self-esteem out of
him, so he does the next best thing and destroys things.'
She laughed unsteadily at the irony of it. 'He dreams of
being an engineer and building bridges, and the same
afternoon I goaded him into telling me that, he slashed
my car tyres.'

Buchanan whistled. 'What did you do?'

'I gave him a bill for the expense,' she said shortly.

'You invoiced the kid?' He gave a guffaw.

'I've worked on him for weeks to agree to some
coaching after school and we were to start on Monday,
and if I don't turn up he'll shrug his shoulders and think,
so what—just one more adult in his life who doesn't give
a damn.'

She turned to find him watching her. 'You should be
more detached. You can care too much.'

'It's just that I can't abide *waste*, you see. Christopher has a perfectly good mind and it's going to waste.'

He grunted. 'Old dumps, young punks—is there anything else you want to save?' He closed his eyes and appeared to forget her.

She roamed around, reading the writing on the wall. 'Malcolm Rules, OK' scrawled in six-inch-high letters, no doubt by someone called Malcolm, had spawned dozens of replies in the same vein. 'Golden Rules, OK' and the quirky 'Amnesia Rules, O...' In a small, feminine hand beneath these was written plaintively, 'Love Rules'.

'Tell me about your travels,' she said, feeling a sudden deepening of the chill. She sat down again and dragged the tattered blanket up to her chin, playing the torch over the posters and graffiti, evidence of other human occupation. 'I suppose you've seen a lot of the world— everywhere they play cricket, anyway.'

He came back from wherever he'd been and looked blankly at her. 'Oh, sure. And a lot of places where they don't. You're not missing as much as you think. One place is much like another.'

'That's very cynical.'

He shrugged. 'Have you been anywhere at all?'

She sighed. 'All around Australia from Ayers Rock to Wagga Wagga and twice to the States, but that was with my parents when I was too young to appreciate it. After I turned twelve I stayed with my aunt and uncle whenever my parents went away. Since then I haven't travelled.' But only because she'd refused the lavish offers of air tickets from her parents, insisting on her independence. He didn't ask why her parents travelled so much.

He pulled on the blanket, removing her hand clutched to its edge. She had herself more or less under control but couldn't stop the tremor in her limbs. Sam must have felt it for he held on to her wrist for a moment then sighed and said, 'OK. Where do you want to go?'

'Go?'

'I can take you to England, India, Sri Lanka, New
Zealand, the West Indies or France, Canada, Malaysia—
where to, Charlotte Wells?'

Charlotte blinked at him. Even to stop a cellmate from
hysterics, she wouldn't have thought Sam Buchanan
would be the type to indulge in flights of fancy. For the
first time Charlotte warmed to him. 'Hmm. New Zealand
would be nice. Or France. Paris. Have you been to
Paris?'

'Several times.' He grimaced, said with an air of reluctance, 'It has to be Paris, I suppose.'

'Not if you'd rather not,' she said, with interest. 'But
I thought you said one place was much the same as
another.'

'Yeah,' he growled and took the torch from her, turned
it off. In the dark, he talked about Paris hotels and the
Eiffel Tower and the number of steps inside the Arc de
Triomphe. Paris by night. It sounded like the com-
mentary for slides, but there were no pictures and his
words created none for her. The way he told it, Paris,
city of lovers, was dead as a doornail. Charlotte's mind
wandered. To daredevil Gale who would spend this night
of Friday the thirteenth artificially frightening herself to
death by watching horror movies, while her conservative
cousin was entombed in a cellar with the tall, dark
stranger of Gale's dreams. To her parents, who were
probably putting down the first tracks for their next
album and wouldn't think of her. Back to Sam Buchanan
and this single bunk and the lone blanket and the long,
cold night ahead.

'—tour boats along the Seine. They're called *bateaux
mouches*,' Sam said, and paused a moment. 'Do you
want to hear about London now?'

Charlotte shuddered. 'No, thanks,' she said a bit too
forcefully. The torch snapped on, shone in her face.

'What's the matter? You wanted to know about the
places you haven't seen and I'm telling you,' he said with
the injured air of a man rejected in a rare moment of

generosity. Charlotte turned her face irritably from the
light.

'I want to know about them—I don't want to be
present at their burial!' She pushed away his hand with
the torch.

'For Pete's sake—you ungrateful little——' he exclaimed. 'I was only talking to stop you getting hysterical again. Don't expect any sympathy from me, angel,
if you start screeching.'

'I appreciate your effort to take my mind off things,
but I don't want the whole world spoiled by your
cynicism, thank you very much, even if I *never* get to
see it!'

'Angel, that's just fine with me. Let's share one of
those dinky little sandwiches of yours and get some sleep.'

Eating didn't take long. He turned off the torch,
turned on the lamp. 'Just for a few minutes,' Sam said.
'Better not waste the batteries, just in case.' Long
shadows stretched across the floor and crookedly up the
walls. The pop stars stared out of their posters like pris-
oners from their cell windows. The makeshift meal finished, she busied herself tidying up her knapsack, re-
screwing the vacuum flask lid, blowing dust off her
lunch-box lid. Sam folded his arms, leaned back against
the wall and watched her. For the first time since she'd
left home that morning she gave some thought to her
appearance. No doubt she looked a mess. Her fair hair,
baby-fine and straight, was wisping from the elastic band
that held it into a pony-tail and her face was probably
streaked with dirt and dust. It maddened her that here,
in this deathtrap of a place, she felt the urge to tidy her
hair because he was looking. But she resisted it.

The stretcher was looking narrower than ever.
Charlotte furtively looked around for a stray mattress
or a moth-eaten old sleeping bag she might have missed.
Sam read all these signals correctly.

'If you think I'm going to be the big hero and sleep
on the floor while you're tucked up in bed, forget it,'

he said. 'There's one bunk and one blanket and I intend to use both, with you or without you, understand?'

'Clearly.' She sent him a withering look.

'Chivalry is dead,' he said, unabashed. 'Don't be misled by all that sunshine today. It's going to be a long, cold night, believe me. I've spent twenty of them wrapped up in a sleeping-bag with a minus ten degree rating.' He snapped off the lamp, turned on the tiny torch and pointed it at the bed. 'Shall we?'

'You can have the stretcher,' she said, talking fast. 'I very much doubt that I'll be able to sleep anyway; I'll sit on one of these boxes——' She grabbed one of the fruit crates, dragged it across the stone floor. It made a high pitched screech like chalk on a shiny blackboard. Sam frowned at all this activity. He studied her for a moment or two.

'You said you'd been waiting for the right man...does that mean you've never shared a bed with a man before? Is that why you're like a cat on hot bricks?' When she didn't answer he sighed, then came over and clamped a hand around her arm, hauling her up from the austerity of the crate. 'Relax,' he said, wheeling her over to the stretcher and dumping her there with about as much interest as if she'd been a sack of potatoes. 'Not all of us are mindless jocks. Incredible as it might seem, I can share a bed with a female body without losing control. Personally, I have to *like* the female first, and I sure as hell have to like the body——' The torch light lingered derisively on the lack of substance beneath her shirt, dismissively over her baggy shorts and down her ultra-slim legs. 'So far I'm not frothing at the mouth,' he said drily.

Charlotte flushed at this cavalier treatment. So he didn't fancy her. Good. But it seemed a flimsy protection against unwelcome attentions. If he had fancied her, then what? Charlotte would have preferred to believe she could relax because he would respect her rights as a person, not because she wasn't his type.

'Suspicious, aren't you, angel? First you think I'm chasing you on the bike to have my wicked way with you and now you think my libido is so stimulated by disaster that I'm not safe to sleep with. You're like one of those Victorian maidens, vicariously consumed with matters of sex.'

'Well, you're the expert on vicariousness,' she retorted.

'What?'

'The Champions Catalogue and the Champions Calendar are choice examples. Can't you sell golf clubs and snow skis without pictures of girls in string bikinis?'

'The day men stop paying attention to female anatomy is the day it will stop being used to sell things.'

'And what percentage of your buyers are women? Who buys all the kids' sports gear—the football boots and netball skirts and hockey sticks? Mothers do. Do you suppose they want a calendar of sex kittens hanging in the kitchen? I speak to a lot of mothers and, I can tell you, they don't.'

He looked incredulous. 'How the hell do we get to be talking about my company's marketing strategies? Let's go to bed.' He swept the torch over her. 'And you can take those off if you're sleeping with me.'

'What?' She jerked her hands downwards, not quite certain just what area they had to protect. His saturnine expression was marked as the light steadied on her feet.

'The boots,' he specified. 'I'm not sharing with them.'

He was plainly counting her nervous reaction as proof of his Victorian maiden theory. The trouble with men was, Charlotte thought, they couldn't understand the peculiar vulnerability of being a woman. Casting him a dire look, Charlotte sat on the edge of the bunk and unlaced her boots.

'Army surplus?' he enquired. He picked up a boot and flexed it, squinted down at her foot. 'A size too big for you and they're men's boots, too heavy. Damned fool thing to economise on.'

'They're perfectly good boots,' she said.

'I'll bet they hurt like hell.'

She didn't answer. If it hadn't been for her feet hurting and losing her way, she wouldn't have gone to the creek and probably wouldn't be here now. That made her cheap boots very expensive. Self-consciously she lay down on the edge of the stretcher. The light went out and it was so dark she wasn't sure if her eyes were open or shut. A despairing creak rose from the bed frame as it took Sam's weight. Charlotte found herself jostled over the edge. 'It's narrower than I thought,' he muttered against the back of her neck. 'Too narrow to hold grudges, angel.' A muscular arm swept around her from behind, dislodged her from the bony edge of the bed and tucked her firmly against him. His other arm slid beneath and automatically she raised herself to make it easier. His knees pushed forward and she bent her legs to accommodate the move. He tented the threadbare blanket over them and automatically she took the corner he thrust towards her. It was a bit like dancing—he led and she followed. Apart from those polite moves of co-operation, Charlotte didn't move a muscle. Sam shuffled and twitched, adjusted the angle of his body minutely and disturbingly to hers a dozen times until at last he appeared resigned. A deep sigh riffled in her hair, his ribcage heaved against her back then he was still for a few moments.

'For pity's sake,' he growled at length, prodding her rigid arm. 'Do you have to lie there like a virgin waiting to be sacrificed? I thought we'd dispensed with that.'

'Do you have to be so crude? I'm a little tense, that's all. It's my first time buried alive in a cellar.'

'We're virgins together where that's concerned, angel,' he said wryly. 'Loosen up, will you? You're making me damned uncomfortable.'

'How thoughtless of me!'

His chest heaved. Her ear warmed to a huff of his breath. Charlotte found the faint vibrations of his amusement pleasant. He radiated a steady, solid warmth

that soaked into her. Her feelings of vulnerability faded
a little, yet paradoxically she felt unsafe in a way she
couldn't explain.

'How old are you, angel?'

'I've aged fifty years today, which makes me nearly
seventy-three.'

She felt the muscles of his face pull into a smile. 'I'm
curious. At your age, how come you're—inexperienced?'

Charlotte tensed again. 'If that was true—and I'm not
saying whether it is or isn't—I don't see why you should
sound so incredulous.'

'I'm a cynic.'

'There are some discriminating people around, as you
yourself reminded me. Not everyone goes mindlessly
along with the modern obsession with everything
physical.'

'But even so—to hold out so long. Nearly seventy-
three!' He gave a whistle.

She was startled into laughter.

'Any special reason, angel? You weren't a novice nun,
or something like that?'

All amusement vanished. 'No,' she snapped.

'This boyfriend—what was his name—Brian. Hasn't
he—er—made any moves?'

Her silence would have frozen off a more sensitive
soul. Sam was unperturbed. He seemed intrigued by her
lack of love-life, determined to find a logical reason for
it. Perhaps it was a peculiarity in these times of self-
gratification and disposable relationships. Sometimes
Charlotte felt she was an alien in social terms and wasn't
sure how it had happened. She had never made any resolution to save herself. Countless opportunities had come
her way—been, in fact, almost thrust upon her. Nice
men, attractive men had coaxed and persuaded, but
puzzlingly there was always something missing, she didn't
know what. In the end some of the nice, attractive men
had graduated from persuasion to demand, and some
to outright accusations of frigidity or the insulting,

'What's the matter, don't you like men?' So here she was, twenty-two and still not sure what it was she was waiting for. And maybe even a chance that she might never find out.

'Maybe you have great strength of character,' Sam speculated. 'Or no sex drive? Maybe Brian's got no sex appeal.'

She resisted an urge to defend Brian's sex appeal.

'If this is an effort to distract me from more hysterics, Sam,' she said levelly, 'I have to say I prefer your lack-lustre Paris.' To tell the truth, she couldn't think of any-thing to say in defence of Brian's sex appeal to this stranger who positively exuded it. It was such a trivial thought that she felt ashamed. To her relief, Sam had nothing further to say on the subject.

The night grew colder by the minute. They shivered beneath the dusty, thin blanket, tucked their cold hands under arms and elbows and clung together, grateful for each other's body-heat. She felt a false kind of affection for Sam just for being there and for being alive and warm. He was rough around the edges, chauvinistic, rude and had all the usual self-orientation of a star, but she could be stranded with worse, she supposed.

A faint scrabbling came from above. Dust trickled in the rubble heap. Cockroaches scurried over walls and floor.

'Where's the torch?' she whispered.

'Scared of the dark, angel?' he said, all male tolerance.

'I wanted to look—there might be mice or rats——'

He went rigid. 'Rats?' he said in a hollow voice.

'Scared of rats, Sam?' she mocked. Another moan from the stretcher as Sam raised himself on one elbow and flashed the torch into every corner. 'You *are* scared!' She intercepted a ferocious scowl. 'Relax.' She smiled, much more at home with a man who was scared of something. 'We'll hear them coming. And their eyes gleam red in the dark.'

In the dark again, he took a deep, shuddering breath that nearly pushed Charlotte off the bed. 'My name is mud, my marriage is over, I've lost my kid and just when I thought things couldn't get any worse I get stuck with a gabby blonde in army boots, a lousy bed and maybe rats!'

'Thank you, I'd prefer not to be characterised as a "gabby blonde"—oh. Your kid? You have a child? You're a father?' she said idiotically, trying to super-impose the image of parent over his scruffy sex-appeal and the newspaper images of man-about-town. She couldn't remember reading anything about a child. But then her interest in him didn't date back very far.

'Son. Four years old. Lives with his mother. Steven,' he rapped out. Then after a moment he added, 'Stevie,' and in the diminutive was revealed the raw hurt of a disenfranchised father. He closed up immediately as if realising that he'd given away more than he'd intended. Charlotte pictured him scowling in the dark and was at a loss, taken aback by her rapidly changing opinion of him. From a bad-tempered, swaggering, self-contained male he had metamorphosed into a real man with fears and bruises. The quality of his silence suggested that he regretted his confidences and would make no more and now she was curious.

'Is he smart—Stevie?' she asked. As a topic to get a parent talking she had never known it to fail. In bursts between long silences, then with more eloquence, he shared all the early signs of Stevie Buchanan's genius. His first word spoken at eleven months, his extra-ordinary acumen at two years, his outstanding physical co-ordination at three years.

'He has a miniature cricket bat. The first time I bowled to him, he hit it high and wide. The kindergarten equi-valent of six runs,' he said, reminiscently.

'At this point I think I should tell you that I find cricket a bore,' she warned. 'Just in case this anecdote leads into a blow-by-blow account of how the wickets fell in your best matches.'

'I'll save my best matches as an antidote.'

'To what?'

'Your historical lectures.' He smiled, she was sure of it and wondered how she knew. 'Checkmate, angel.'

When she'd first set eyes on him this morning she wouldn't have thought he had much humour in him. Images of the morning crowded in behind the thought. Of green water and blinding sunlight and him throwing back his head to release a great arc of droplets. She tried to remember when she'd ever been so dumbstruck by mere physical presence. It wasn't as if she hadn't been exposed to scruffy glamour before. Her parents' drummer was an unshaven, unkempt Heathcliff type with superb teeth and a chest so admired that he rarely covered it. Charlotte tried to bring Quinn's image to mind and failed.

'Goodnight, angel. Charlotte.' After a moment he amended, 'Charlie. You don't mind if I call you Charlie?'

'Not at all, Sam. Sammy.'

He chuckled. It was amazing, she thought, that they'd found anything to laugh about in the circumstances. Lying there, nested in against Sam's big body, his hand gradually relaxing on her midriff, his breath stirring the hair on her neck, she knew she wouldn't sleep. Her nerves jangled from the obvious danger and from that other, less defined one. Charlie. She really didn't mind the way he said it. His breathing deepened into an even, hypnotic rhythm and after a while she slept too.

She woke and reached for her bedside clock. It wasn't there. What had happened to her bedside clock? Gale had probably borrowed it. Gale was the absolute limit. She closed her eyes listening to the steady sound of her own breathing, then opened them again. No clock. No bookshelves, no striped wallpaper. Even Gale couldn't borrow the wallpaper. The steady breathing went on somewhere behind her and a dead weight lay across her legs. There was someone in bed with her.

Not since childhood had Charlotte woken in a bed with someone else. Then she had often found herself in her parents' bed where she had fled for refuge from bad dreams. Whatever else Martin and Linda might have lacked as parents, their casual, uncritical acceptance of her fears had been comforting. Never did they say, 'you're too old to be worried about monsters' or 'it's time you were a big girl and stayed in your own bed'. When they woke and found her in their bed they smiled and tickled her and played silly word games, but she always knew that they forgot about her the moment she left the room. Sometimes, if they got to talking about a new synthesizer for the band or a great opening riff for a song, they forgot her even before that.

The dead weight pinning her down was a muscular, masculine leg. An equally muscular arm was draped loosely around her from behind and a broad, deep shoulder loomed on her peripheral vision. She felt overwhelmed by so much maleness, as if she'd shrunk during the night. A few furtive moves failed to dislodge either his arm or leg and she lay there, as entwined with Sam as any figure on an Indian mural, with a growing feeling of claustrophobia. A less subtle shove at his arm made him stir, but only to hook his leg more securely over hers and plant a hand firmly on her stomach. 'Mmmmm,' he mumbled against her neck, scrubbing his bristly chin from side to side, sending tingles halfway down her back. A sultry, tropical heat emanated from Sam and she wondered if she had imagined the freezing temperatures of the night. His hand slid up and closed with authority on her breast. She gave a small gasp of surprise.

'Mmmmmm,' Sam mumbled again with a satisfied sound. Coldly, she took a grip on his wrist and pushed. But a moment later his hand was back, settling itself smugly with a series of little twitches and tweaks. His thumb circled idly and though there was the sturdy cotton of her bra and bush shirt between his touch and her skin, the sensation was astounding, a wave of pleasure rippling through her body. Charlotte flushed at this treacherous response to a caress not even meant for her. He was asleep and she could be just any woman. Any body. It occurred to her that she would feel slightly less outraged if he knew it was her, Charlotte. Her flush deepened as she tried to edge off the bed but with a deep growl Sam hitched her back close against him. Charlotte sucked in her breath sharply, shaken by the clear evidence of his arousal. Somehow she knew he was still asleep, and she knew, too, when he woke only a few moments later.

What to do, what to say? Charlotte couldn't think of anything that wouldn't make things more awkward. She closed her eyes, made her breathing slow and deep. If he didn't hear the kettle-drum beat of her heart, he would think she was still asleep. Behind her, Sam went through various stages of awareness—he nuzzled into her neck and she felt the flick of his eyelashes as he opened his eyes suddenly. About now he was realising that he wasn't dreaming or that she wasn't the woman he usually woke up with. After that came the discovery that his hands were leading a life of their own. He jerked them away from her with a muttered, 'What the hell——?'

There was another muffled curse and this time his body jerked away from her. 'Buchanan, you bloody adolescent——' she heard him mutter. She imagined his ferocious frown and fought back a giggle.

'You awake, Charlie?' he said cautiously, after a moment.

'Um,' she mumbled, re-enacting her earlier awakening. She turned a little and opened her eyes to a stunning close-up view of Sam's mouth and stubbly jaw. Shadows defined his cheekbones and the concave plane of one cheek. The scarred eyebrow quirked in its permanent mockery. He was familiar, but a stranger, and she'd spent the night in his arms. Sam hovered over her looking just a touch anxious, she thought, liking him for it.

'Oh,' she said lamely, surprised by this sudden warmth of feeling she felt for him. 'You look like a desperado.'

His blue eyes studied her for a moment or two. Probably comparing her to the kind of woman who usually prompted such early morning enthusiasm, she thought on a sudden sour note. Sam ran the heel of his hand down his bristling jaw.

'Yeah. I feel like a desperado.'

'How did you get those scars?' Too late she realised she'd referred to the scar not on display—the one she'd seen yesterday when he was naked.

'For someone crazed with fear, you got a good look, angel,' he said, a gleam in his eyes. 'This one,' he said, patting his ribs, 'was a water-skiing accident. And I took a bouncing delivery on my forehead—I was nineteen and, being macho, batting without a helmet. It cured me. I've worn a helmet since.'

It hadn't cured him of being macho. He was just naturally, overwhelmingly so. Charlotte had never been so close to a man with so much personal magnetism. For a moment longer he stayed there, looking down at her then got up, turned his back to tuck in his T-shirt and did some warm-up stretches followed by star jumps and running on the spot. It was clear he was favouring his left leg.

'You talked in your sleep,' he told her, turning to face her again.

'What did I say?'

He gripped his wrists with his hands and did some isometric exercises. Even in the dim grey light, Charlotte could see his chest muscles flexing beneath his T-shirt. 'This and that—something about a Roman god in the creek.' He smirked.

Charlotte regarded him with less favour. Conceited oaf. He might have had the diplomacy not to mention it, considering what he'd been doing while *he* was asleep.

'I must have been dreaming. I was having a dream before I woke just now, as a matter of fact,' she said, puckering her brow as if trying to recall it. Out of the corner of her eye she saw Sam abruptly abandon his exercises. 'I can't quite remember what it was about, except that—er——'

'What?' he said, hands tensely on his hips.

'It was horrible.'

CHAPTER FOUR

'"FORGET the notes and play the music",' Charlotte read from the wall. Half the day had passed in grinding slowness as they took turns to stand on the crates and chip mortar from a block above ground level. Her neck and shoulders aching from her stint, Charlotte was taking a break while Sam tapped away with a half-brick and a short length of metal. '"Hummingbirds have forgotton the words". That's almost poetic but forgotten is misspelled. I must tell that one to my father. He's always looking for——'

For new ideas for lyrics. Poetic phrases, unusual word combinations. Earthbound was known for the intelligence and beauty of its lyrics. Rock and roll for grown-ups.

'Looking for what?' Sam prompted.

Charlotte hesitated over telling Sam about her parents. Once people knew, it tended to dominate the conversation and overshadow Charlotte Wells, schoolteacher.

'Oh, odd facts—you know,' she said vaguely. 'I wonder who carved the writing on the tree down by the creek? "Robert and Emma. Journeys end in lovers meeting." It's a quotation from *Twelfth Night.*'

'My education is complete,' he mocked. 'Did Bob and Emma get their spelling right, teach? Will you give them ten out of ten?'

'You have a rotten disposition.'

'It's being trapped with a teacher. It does it every time. You remind me of a dragon who taught me in seventh grade, Miss Penrose. Used to purse up her mouth the way you do when she saw the wrong spelling. Used to look over her glasses at me with X-ray eyes. "Samuel Buchanan," she would say, "being able to run very fast

57

and throw a ball accurately does not equip you for life. Pay attention.'''

She was dismayed by his mimicry of a prissy, elderly Miss Penrose. 'I'm too young to be characterised as a dragon,' she said shortly.

'Dragons evolve. She might have been a lot like you when she was young.'

Charlotte sent him a look of profound dislike that seemed to restore his humour. For something to do, she began to unravel the tangled bits of string and copper left behind by a previous tenant. The feeling of helplessness drove her crazy. Earlier they had ripped another poster from the wall and torn it into quarters. On the back of each they had written an SOS note giving the date and place they were trapped. Then Sam had hoisted Charlotte up to each air vent in turn until they found one with a rusting outside grate. Held aloft on Sam's shoulders, she'd stabbed through the aperture until the mesh crumbled, then poked the notes through. 'I can see sunlight on grass,' she'd told Sam wistfully, leaning forward to prolong this glimpse of the outside world. 'One of the notes has just blown away in the wind.' She set her eye, birdlike, to the vent. 'There's a dandelion growing there. A ladybird is crawling up the stem.'

'I needed to know that,' Sam had said sourly and, clamping his hands on her thighs, brought her down. It had been a smooth descent but rough on her nerves. She'd felt the bite of his long fingers, the pleasant roughness of his palms along the length of her legs and wished she were wearing jeans. Damn you, Gale, she'd thought, making it to the ground in a breathless state.

After that, Sam had rolled out the abandoned copper lid and some lengths of rusting pipe and crouched, gazing at them, muttering under his breath.

'What's that for?' she'd asked.

'Quiet. I'm cogitating.'

Now the lengths of knotted string yielded at last and she held up the results of her patient work. 'Look,' she said. 'Wind chimes.'

'Thank God,' Sam said fervently. 'We've got a chance of survival now we've found the wind chimes.'

The day passed and no one came. They made a dent in the mortar that made them depressingly aware that it would take weeks, months even, to scratch out enough to loosen a stone. As the daylight softened towards sunset, Charlotte stood on the bunk and hung the wind chimes on a blackened ceiling hook. From time to time as she paced about, reading bits of graffiti, she stirred them, making them shimmer and jingle.

'"Down with gravity",' she read from the wall. 'Clever. "Down with beer". "Down with escelaters".' Escalators was mispelled. Absently she stroked the chimes again. 'What message would you leave on the wall, Sam?'

He didn't hesitate. 'Down with wind chimes.'

The call of crows and the evening bird chorus came to them. They ate their meagre evening rations in silence. Afterwards, as the light went and the cellar greyed, Sam got up and paced. Four paces from the bunk, four paces back. He must have marked and cleared his course while it was still light, because he didn't fall over anything. She lay on the stretcher. It was the worst time of the day, too dark to do anything, too early for sleep. Perhaps, she thought, this was how it had been in more primitive times. An interval for thinking, between work and sleep. With artificial lighting, radio, television and the myriad other distractions of civilisation, humans could avoid just thinking for years, maybe all their lives. She could see why they did it. Without distractions you were forced to be honest with yourself, admit your fears, look at all the stupid things you did. Like wishing your parents were ordinary people and fussed over you. Like being attracted to Sam Buchanan. Four paces away, four

paces back. It got on her nerves. At last she burst out,
'Why don't you sit down or come to——?'

Sam stopped. 'Come to bed?'

'Get some sleep,' she said, going for a less intimate
phrase.

He laughed. 'I've never known anyone so careful with
words. You act as if they're Molotov cocktails—throw
the wrong one in and all hell might break loose. Do you
think I might get all worked up if you say "come to
bed"?'

'Common usage changes some phrases,' she said with
dignity. 'And some words *are* Molotov cocktails—you
ought to know.'

Sam sat heavily on the edge of the bunk. 'Yeah,' he
said with a sigh. 'I guess I've thrown a few lately.'

'That story about the nude girl in your hotel room,'
she said tentatively.

'You want to know if it's true? Of course it's true. It
was in the newspapers, wasn't it?' he mocked. 'Some
nutty little sports groupie bribes her way into my hotel
room, whips off her gear and waits for me. I get photographed trying to usher her out, I say I don't even
know the girl's name—absolutely true. I come out of
the thing looking like some insensitive jock.'

'And what about Sam Buchanan, drunk in a nightclub,
pushing photographers around?'

He inched her aside, stretched out on his back then
casually scooped her close so that she lay front-down,
half on the canvas, half on him. A hot and cold situation. Her face found its natural position somewhere in
the curve of his shoulder. A slight move and her mouth
encountered stubbled neck. Another and his hair tickled
her nose. Surely, she thought crossly, there was some
small, bland, untextured part of him that didn't scrape
or irritate or deliver mild electric shocks. She managed
to get an elbow on to the canvas and propped her head
up on her hand, safely out of range. Safely? A hilarious

word to use in the circumstances. A hilarious word to use about Sam Buchanan at any time.

'Sam Buchanan, drunk,' he said flatly, as if he was talking about someone else. 'Ruth had slapped a court order on me that day, denying me access to Stevie. I didn't take it like a man, I'm afraid,' he said in self-deprecation. 'I went out with some mates to drown my sorrows, tagged along with them when they went on to a nightclub. And I didn't push the photographer around, just stopped him shoving the camera in my face. He said a few words to me, I said a few back——'

'Molotov cocktails for two?'

'Mm. A twelve-year-old kid mailed his poster back to me, torn into little pieces after that nightclub episode. Even Mrs Hume's sulking about it—she's my house-keeper—goes around giving me accusing looks and sniffing all the time. Bloody silly woman. She would go putting me on a pedestal. Sooner or later I was bound to fall off.' There was resentment in him for all the people who put him on pedestals and maybe anger with himself for falling off.

'Heroes have a limited life,' she said. 'The perfect hero is the one who dies young—never gets a chance to make a mess of things, never gets inexcusably old and wrinkled, never——' She caught in her breath sharply, suddenly realising what she was saying.

'If dying young would help my image, Grahame would have thought of it,' he said drily. 'Bad press for me means less credibility for Champions. Grahame occupies himself with plans to restore me to my pedestal.'

'No wonder he looks tense,' she said, trying to hold back the tremor of fear. 'Does he know you've shaved off the company logo?'

He laughed and she heard the rasp as he fingered the site of the former moustache. 'No.'

'Will you re-grow it if—when we get out of here?'

'Probably not. Might be time for a change.' After a moment he took her hand, gave it a squeeze. 'I thought we might do Paris again. What do you say?'

Sam's hand holding hers was great therapy. How nice of him to quietly offer comfort. There was more to Sam than met the eye and that was saying plenty. 'None of that jaded stuff—strictly your first impression?'

'Never seen the place before in my life. We've just arrived, OK.'

With Sam's arm about her, she listened while he made his way back to his first impression of Paris, before every place became much like another. This tour was not like that dry, factual account he'd served up last night. Tonight he reached back and found the pictures he'd seen himself and recreated them for her. The traffic lurching around the Arc de Triomphe like the chariots out of Ben Hur, so that tourists gathered and crossed the road in convoys for safety. The tower-tall Africans selling flying mechanical birds under the Eiffel, the man in baggy pants in the Tuileries Gardens trailed by a flock of sparrows that flew up one by one at his command to take seed from his hand. Buskers—a boy with a violin and a girl with wild, curling hair playing a flute, collecting coins in a black bowler hat in the Metro underground. 'I wonder whatever happened to them ... the happiest couple.' Which happiest couple did he mean, Charlotte wondered, the buskers or himself and whoever had shared his first impressions of Paris?

'The Louvre is closed,' Sam said.

'Oh, darn!'

'We'll go tomorrow. Tonight we go dancing——' The stretcher creaked and groaned as Sam got up and pulled her into his arms. He hummed an old Stevie Wonder song, whirled her around once within his four-pace area and then came to halt in a clumsy way as if he'd suddenly forgotten how to do it. 'No music,' he said. 'Let's go to bed.' His fingers clicked. 'Sorry. I mean, let's get some sleep.'

When they were settled under the blanket, Charlotte said, 'I liked tonight's Paris. It must have been fun.'

'Yes. I'd forgotten the way it was...' He raised her hand, pressed a careless, whiskery kiss on it as if remembering Paris had roused some Gallic instinct in him. 'Goodnight, Charlie.'

She was still awake when he fell asleep. Charlotte had a feeling that, somewhere in the streets of Paris, she'd substituted for someone else. His ex-wife, perhaps. The strangest feeling surged through her. Indignation that he might have forgotten her in the dark, and envy for the woman who'd shared his days of innocence. In the pitch black she closed her eyes on the pictures of Paris he'd created for her and questioned her advice to her students. In every adversity there was always a positive. Or it could simply look that way.

Sam woke in the mood for love. He lay very still, Charlotte's hair in his face and her bare, silky thigh beneath his palm. Reluctantly he removed his hands from her and slid from the bed, anxious not to wake her. He held the blanket up for a moment to study her. With or without the army boots she had great legs. Letting the blanket drop, he softfooted a short distance from the bed and began some strenuous floor exercises. The morning light, filtering down through the debris, was a soft, grey fog but he could see Charlotte well enough as he sweated over his sit-ups. Wryly he wondered how the hell he found himself in this situation. It was as if Charlotte triggered off memories of better times—like last night. For the first time in years he'd felt young and carefree again. He'd taken out several beautiful, willing women these past six months and failed to whip up any excitement over them, yet here he was in disastrous circumstances fancying a girl who was a cross between Joan of Arc and his fifth-grade history teacher. Stuck in a lousy, rotten place with no way out, he felt in some ways more alive than he had for a year.

Charlotte stretched out an arm and rolled on to her side. Her cardigan was twisted up behind her and her bush shirt had come unbuttoned while she slept and he was offered a tantalising view of her breasts. Why tantalising, he couldn't fathom. She wasn't exactly over-abundant in that department and she wore a sensible white cotton bra that didn't reveal much. Maybe it was because he knew he wasn't meant to see it. Maybe in a world gone mad with a surfeit of peekaboo lace and satin and the conscious display of the female body, the accidental glimpse of a cotton bra was a novelty. He thought of the Champions calendar and the twelve glorious, underdressed girls who would mark the months decked out with skis or scuba tanks or football boots. It left him unmoved. It had left him unmoved for a long time, he realised now, along with a lot of other things, like Champions itself, which had been such a challenge in the building but failed now to excite him. Sam was conscious of a new restlessness that had nothing to do with his downhill sporting career.

Charlotte rolled over and her shirt gaped down to her shorts waistband. He couldn't explain why Charlotte attracted him. She wasn't, after all, the kind of girl to send the blood rushing to a man's head. He gave a crooked grin. She sent it rushing, but not to his head. Sam jogged energetically. Charlotte woke and looked over at him as he raised dust with some serious star-jumps. He waited for her to complain about the dust but she just covered a sneeze with one hand, pushed back her hair and smiled at him. 'Good morning.'

Sam was irked. What was she smiling at? She looked almost tolerant, as if she knew what he was sublimating with all this activity. 'Morning,' he said brusquely, reminding himself that she was the reason they were in this mess.

His temper didn't improve. Today Charlotte irritated him with her stiff-upper-lip cheerfulness and her almost ceremonial sharing out of a slice of fruit cake. He hated fruit cake. She was back with the historical notes in that clear, precise voice.

'Everyone said Henry Hawker wouldn't be able to grow grapes here, but he was determined and proved them all wrong,' she said chattily. Schoolteacher through and through. Sam tried to think of a teacher he'd ever really liked.

'The vines died from some disease, you said.'

'Phylloxera, yes. But not before he'd had four good vintages.'

'What a shame for Harry.'

'Later, his son—I think his name was Thomas——'

'How could I forget old Tom?'

He could see she made a big effort to ignore his irreverence with the names. 'Anyway, Thomas and *his* son, Richard, started the vineyard up again but the vines failed. They planted the apple orchard but all the trees died, so they had to replant with a different variety. Those trees are still there today.'

'Poor old Tom, Dick and Harry,' he mocked. 'All that effort and what's left? A mouldy old ruin and a few apple trees.'

Charlotte's lips pressed together in disapproval. 'What a waste. Why couldn't Cranston have been inherited by someone with the foresight and the—the courage to build on the past instead of tearing it down?' she said. 'You have a wrecker's mentality. If something sags in the middle—get rid of it!'

'Sags in the middle?' he derided. 'The place has come down around our *ears*, angel!'

'Only some of it,' she said and went on to deliver a lecture about the glorious staircase, the cedar joinery, the unusual keystone arched windows. She rabbited on about shoring the house up, strengthening it with some discreet steel beams before rebuilding the roof, and he let her finish then said flatly, but with malicious anticipation, 'I've already arranged for the wreckers to give me a quote. The minute I get out of here, the bulldozers come in.'

Her response was all he could have wished. She gave a hurt little gasp as if he'd threatened her personally. And there was a blessed silence for at least thirty seconds before she started again.

'Maybe you should let Cranston moulder on for another twenty years and give it to your son. After all, it's *his* inheritance too.'

'Then *he'd* bulldoze it to the ground.'

She was breathing hard. He was angry but fascinated. When was the last time he'd seen a woman who cared so much about something that didn't benefit herself? Sam felt suddenly intimidated by her. You had some bargaining power with a woman who wanted jewellery and cars and seaside villas.

'You lash out at everything, don't you, Sam? Umpires, photographers. But your son comes from a long line of people who knew how to build things, not knock them down. Who knows? If he grows up without you around, he might turn out to be a builder instead of a wrecker!'

It hit him like a blow to the solar plexus. 'Without me around?' Stevie, growing up, turning into a teenager, and him not there every day to listen to him, to play ball with him, take him fishing, teach him how to become a man? She'd felled him with his greatest fear. 'You righteous little bitch,' he said harshly, trying to mask his hurt with anger.

She saw right through it. 'Oh, Sam,' she said at once, moving in to lay her hand on his arm. 'I'm sorry. That was a low blow. You just made me so mad.' She looked up at him, opening those blue-grey eyes wide. 'I didn't mean to hurt you.'

'Hurt?' he said roughly, denying it. 'Infuriate, you mean. For Pete's sake stop looking at me like that.' He grasped her arm and gave her a shake which moved her close.

'Like what?'

'Like an understanding woman.'

She was closer than he thought. Close enough for him to scent that odd fragrance about her that transcended the dust and mustiness of the place. He loosed his hand from her arm for the pleasure of closing it again, letting each fingertip press into the soft flesh.

'I don't know what you've got against understanding women,' she said huskily. With satisfaction he saw that she was no longer giving him the sorrowful gaze that irked him. Charlotte looked, in fact, a bit rattled. That was better. Power surged through his system. He moved his hand up her arm to her shoulder, finding a sharp pleasure in the way she fitted into his palm but more from the scarcely audible catch of her breath.

Joan of Arc was vulnerable. He knew she was attracted to him, of course, had noticed the tiny signals she'd tried to suppress. Here was one subject on which this gabby female was a self-confessed novice. His pride was restored, soothed by the feeling of control. She made no move away when he fingered her other shoulder, brought her a fraction closer.

'Uh——' she said, or some such inarticulate sound that was amusing coming from Charlie, who was never lost for a word, and a big word at that. Sam half smiled and bent, savouring the moment when he'd kiss her, prolonging it. Charlotte ran her tongue over her lips and the nervous, anticipatory movement stoked the warmth low down in his belly. He could tie this prissy little do-gooder up in knots if he wanted. He let his hands skim over her shoulder blades, down to her waist and the starting slopes of that delicious backside hidden away in the baggy shorts.

But, his mouth almost touching hers, he hesitated. Looking into Charlotte's anxious, excited but apprehensive blue-grey eyes, he drew back, feeling like some third-rate actor playing the cad in an old movie. He took his hands off her, shoved them into his jeans pockets out of harm's way. Broodingly, he noticed her top shirt button was undone again and her nice, sensible cotton bra was displaying very small portions of her breasts. The blood rushed from his head in a southerly direction. Like an Edwardian turned on by the glimpse of an ankle, he thought sourly. 'Your buttonholes have stretched,' he told her, and took some short-lived pleasure in her dismay. He watched her produce a tiny sewing kit from that bottomless knapsack. She turned her back on him to repair the stretched buttonholes. She went around carrying a sewing kit, for God's sake! Even his small Edwardian pleasures were to be denied him.

CHAPTER FIVE

THREE days. Sunday. Only the dried fruits and the wine were left of Charlotte's picnic lunch. Half the drinking water remained. Two more posters had gone, fluttering away in fragments, bearing SOS messages that might never be read. The other posters they had taken down and made into notes ready to dispense at intervals. There were spaces where they had been, surrounded by graffiti, looking like faded patches on papered walls in a house whose owner was selling off the family paintings.

'How old were you when you got married, Sam?' Charlotte asked, chipping away at the mortar.

Sam, on his haunches, speculating on new ways to unblock the staircase, looked up. 'What brought that on?'

She shrugged. 'Something to keep my mind off roast lamb with mint sauce, roast potatoes and green peas, fresh fruit salad and lashings of——'

'OK, *OK*,' he groaned. 'I was twenty-two. Too young.' A long silence followed during which Charlotte tapped at the mortar and tried to imagine Sam at her own age. 'Ruth was twenty. She was a top model, I was a sports star. We were both still trying to handle success while most kids are just coping with growing up. I needed some stability—someone to come home to between cricket tours—and she was having a hard time handling the VIP types who proposition young models. I guess we were both relieved to get married and take the heat off. A mutual safe harbour.'

'But you were in love.'

'Head over heels. I'll-love-you-forever stuff. A grand passion. In the beginning, anyway. I don't know what went wrong but in the end the only thing Ruth was

69

passionate about was money,' he said drily, coming over
to take his shift on the wall. He lifted her down and took
the tools from her. 'And no matter how much you have
there's always someone with more.'

It sounded sordid, dreadful. 'Better luck next time,'
she said lamely.

Sam, up on the crates, delivered a belting blow and
mortar crumbled. 'Are you kidding, angel? I'll make
damned sure there's no next time.'

The confessional had a disturbing effect. Sam tapped
away, frowning, as if regretful that he'd said so much,
and Charlotte felt edgy, claustrophobic. The atmosphere had a charged, pre-storm feeling about it.
Charlotte took out her camera gear and a polishing cloth
and cleaned the sparkling lenses. She'd already done it
three times but the repetition was therapeutic.

'Don't include me in any of your pictures,' Sam said
shortly, when she idly raised the Chinon. 'I don't want
to find them plastered all over the weekend papers if we
get out of here.'

Charlotte drew in her breath sharply. Did he think she
would *sell* pictures of him? She swung the camera to
where he stood on the crate, looking like Michelangelo,
chipping away at stone. It would make a fantastic picture,
at that. 'What do you think I'd get for them, Sam? I
could really use a couple of hundred dollars, we teachers
are dreadfully underpaid. Maybe I could write an article
to go with them—"I Bunked with Buchanan".' He
looked down and Charlotte saw his face close up automatically against the intrusion of the camera. The process
wasn't nearly so effective without the moustache. For a
private man in the public eye, that moustache had been
an asset—a decoy to stop too close a scrutiny. Like her,
millions of people had seen the Champions logo and
never really seen the man.

Sam jumped down, slapped dust from his arms. 'No
pictures, angel. I'm not kidding. Put it away.' He came
towards her, a hand outstretched to the camera and she

backed away, pretending to take shots, furious that he would treat her with the same distrust he would a nosy Press photographer.

'Give us a nice, big scowl now, Sam.' The flash unit flared and lit the cellar briefly with a blue-white light. Sam took a hold on the camera and she fought to maintain her grip. As he raised it, she lost contact and the camera flew from his hands, bounced off the wall and skittered across the floor.

'My *camera*——' Charlotte wailed and dived for it, handling the chunky Chinon Genesis with tenderness. The lens was starred, the flash unit snapped off. 'You've wrecked it! I saved for ages for this camera——'

'It was an accident,' he said. 'Invoice me, angel.'

His sarcasm was the last straw. She lashed out at him but he ducked and fielded her flailing hand, carrying it down behind her. The move brought her close enough to see the sudden flare of intent in his eyes.

'Brute,' she said hoarsely. 'Are you going to throw *me* across the room, now?' Charlotte's throat was dry as the dust that hung in the air. The odd sensation of waiting reached a peak. Only the harsh sound of his breath and hers, and the drum of her heartbeat.

Sam bent and pressed his mouth to her neck and everything in her surged forward for the touch, craving it again, as the pleasure of it rippled through her body. *Please*. Charlotte caught her breath, wondering if she'd said that out loud. It alarmed her, threatened the self-discipline on which she prided herself and made her resent this big, angry, experienced male who thought she was someone else every morning. As he tilted her head back and looked at her, eyes glittering, she gathered all her dwindling resolution and turned from his kiss.

'Time for your calisthenics,' she said waspishly, before she thought.

Sam froze. A wash of colour spread over his cheek-bones and his mouth compressed to a hard, ungiving line. Charlotte was remorseful at once. He had taken

pains to spare her embarrassment and here she was
flinging his thoughtfulness back in his face.

'Sam, I didn't mean——' she began, but his frown
was thunderous and his eyes snapped with temper. Still
clutching her camera, she backed away.

'You were awake then, yesterday, were you?' he said
through gritted teeth. 'And this morning too? Faking
sleep and having a good laugh at me, I suppose, while
I've been pussyfooting around trying not to offend your
delicate sense of refinement! Ha, bloody ha! Delicacy!
Talk about a myth. Women have about as much delicacy
as a bull in a bloody china shop!'

'I wasn't having a good laugh—I——'

Sam caught up with her, grasped her arm and swung
her around to thrust his face close to hers. 'Don't imagine I've been turned on because you've got anything
special, will you? You've got a nice body but you're very
average and I'm used to beautiful women, but you know
how it is with us randy, insensitive *jocks*, angel.' He
paused for effect. 'All cats are grey in the dark——'

Charlotte smarted. Her face flamed and she forgot
how sorry she was and kicked him. Her sturdy army
boot thudded into his shin. Sam let out a yell and hopped
on one leg, but he held on to her wrist. Abruptly he
reeled her in and she fetched up against him, her head
flung back, her hands spread on his chest. This time he
gave her no chance to turn away. A glimpse she had of
glowering, furious eyes before he bent to kiss her. An
unforgiving kiss, expert, deliberate, stamping his dom-
inance on the situation. And there was something else
that ran like an electric current beneath the surface. It
proved more powerful than resentment and Sam drew
back for a moment, looked at her through half-closed
eyes then kissed her again, softly, persuasively, dipping
inside in a slow, provocative exploration. The sensation
hummed through her body. She was sliding her arms
around his neck when Sam lifted his head abruptly,
listening.

'What's that?' he asked in a tone so normal that she hated him.

'Well, it's not my madly beating heart,' Charlotte said acidly, hoping it *wasn't* her galloping heartbeat he had picked up. 'If that's what nude groupies chase you for, then all I can say is——' He gagged her with a hand over her mouth and she honked and squirmed but he said, 'Listen!' and she held her breath and listened.

A sharp sound like a cork popping from a bottle. Then a quick volley of sounds.

'Shots!' Sam exclaimed. 'Hunters, after rabbits, I suppose—I saw burrows all along the slopes. Quick—let's shove those notes out through the vent and pray for wind.' He hoisted her up on to his shoulders and she thrust the jigsaw pieces of David Bowie through the vent, using the stick feverishly to push them out where a breeze might disperse them. 'Noise stations, Charlie——' he said, as she slithered down his back. 'You're not short on words—I hope you're as good on volume.' He blew on his hands, seized a club of wood he had put aside for the occasion and squared up to the copper lid he'd dragged into position yesterday. 'This is it, angel! We're getting out of here.'

He lifted the club sideways and delivered a resounding blow to the iron. Charlotte stumbled to the length of drainage pipe he'd positioned pointing upwards to the patch of sky. She screamed like a banshee into the pipe, beat on it with the stick Sam had laid beside it and the bloodcurdling, amplified sound filled the cellar. 'Music to my ears!' Sam bellowed, swinging the club back for another swipe.

After a few minutes they stopped, hot and panting. Sam pulled his T-shirt off, tossed it aside. The shots seemed fainter now and they redoubled their efforts. For almost half an hour they kept it up, taking turns to rest. Sam, muscles bunched and glistening, struck the make-shift gong again and again, like some ancient hammerman sounding the strokes on a slave galley and, when he stopped for a breather, Charlotte beat on the pipe and screamed through it. The sound of shots grew fainter still. Desperation seized them. Sam's blows quickened until he was beating out a battle pace. The lid crumbled in the centre, and still he pounded on it, sending bits of rusting metal flying until it collapsed.

Panting, choking, they stopped. No sound of shots. Only the rasp of their breathing and, a long way off, the rumble of thunder. Sam slumped against the wall. Charlotte crouched down to begin the noise again and he lifted a hand wearily and said, 'Save your breath.' In helpless rage, she beat a last tattoo with the metal rod.

'Bastards!' she shrieked into the pipe. 'Shooting at poor little rabbits! Why don't you pick on something your own size!'

It was then that they heard the dainty sound of raindrops.

'Rain,' Charlotte whispered and sank back on her haunches. Each drop would make a perfect silver circle on the surface of the creek. Dandelion heads would nod and long blades of grass would tremble. The SOS notes, drifting perhaps towards the hunters, would be driven into the grass by the rain, and turn to pulp. The incomparable smell of a rainy spring afternoon reached them and that seemed the final mockery to Charlotte. She sat on the bed and howled and, after a moment, Sam came and held her.

They drank some wine that night. Sipping it from a plastic tumbler in the dark, Charlotte wondered if perhaps subconsciously they had saved it for this moment. The rain had been the forerunner of a storm and they had kept their hopes alive as long as they could. 'The hunters might find your camp and report it,' Charlotte said. 'The storm might drive them up to the house for shelter.' They'd waited and listened and when they thought it was dark enough outside they had shone Charlotte's lamp up through the tiny opening—on, off, on, off—until they realised that, even if the hunting party was still nearby, their signal would appear as just another flicker of lightning. The light was dim when they turned it off, the batteries almost flat.

So they'd let hope go, then. In a way, it was almost a relief. 'We'll drink some wine tonight,' Sam had said, and they had taken turns in the wine alcove, stripping down in the dark to wipe away the dust and grime of their exertions with the dwindling basin water and the cracked sliver of soap and Charlotte's tiny hand towel. Charlotte even patted around in her knapsack pockets for the lipstick that she hadn't used since Friday morning. She combed her hair and left it loose, and rubbed a little sun cream on her skin for the illusion of perfume. She smelled its faint fragrance now as she lifted the plastic cup of wine to her lips.

'I'd give a lot for a shave,' Sam said, audibly stroking his jaw. 'How's that for trivial?'

'I'm wearing lipstick in the dark. That's pretty trivial.'

He touched her face, drew his thumb along her lower lip. How accurately they found each other in total darkness now, Charlotte thought. It was true what they said. If you were deprived of one sense, others sharpened to compensate.

'So you are. Why, Charlie?'

'The same reason you suddenly wanted to shave, I suppose. It's an occasion—wine with dinner. Maybe I should say, wine *for* dinner.'

His laughter was husky and low. Neither of them had much voice left. Sam leaned close and kissed her on the lips, just a dab of a kiss meant to be comforting in the dark. He lingered a moment, speaking against her mouth. 'I like your lipstick, angel.' Abruptly he withdrew. 'Cheers,' he said, drinking from the bottle. An odd headiness caught Charlotte by surprise. She giggled.

'I think I could be drunk.'

'Impossible. You've had one tumbler of wine.'

'Ah, but usually I never drink on an empty stomach and you have to concede that my stomach could hardly be emptier. It would be the first time I was drunk.' Charlotte thought about that for a moment and added seriously, 'And quite possibly the last.'

Sam clamped his arms around her waist. 'Don't say it. Don't think it.' And he pressed another kiss fiercely to her mouth as if to erase the depressing words. If it was meant to encourage, it succeeded. Optimism glowed in the quiet despair within her. She felt suddenly as if she'd been handed everything she wanted and she kissed him back.

'Steady, Charlie,' he said, pulling away. The bunk creaked as he stood.

'Where are you going?' she asked.

'A nice little harbour restaurant that does a great seafood entrée, I thought, then on to a show at the Opera House——' he drawled. 'Where the hell do you think I'd be going in this lousy cellar?'

'There's no need to be sarcastic. I just—well, we had a nice mood going——'

'Exactly.' There were a few soft thuds.

'What are you doing?'

'Calisthenics,' he said drily.

Charlotte found the pencil torch and shone it at him. He gave her a crooked smile and turned his back to jog on the spot, lifting his knees high. A weird little thrill ran down her spine. Such a beautiful, long, muscled back he had. The line of his spine showed through his T-shirt. She wanted to run her fingertips down it ... the need to touch him was so strong, it rocked her.

'I'd prefer to make love to you, Charlie,' he said bluntly. 'And I have the advantage.' He paused and she wanted to dispute this arrogant statement but couldn't. 'You're attracted to me and I could play on that, but——'

'But——?'

'Well, if I were a woman stuck here with a man I liked I might not feel I could say no if he made a move. After all, he might take rejection badly and make a miserable situation even worse and I might feel—mmm—some obligation to be—nice. If I were a girl, Charlie—your kind of girl—I might not want that kind of complication at a time like this.'

She stared. So Sam Buchanan had been able to imagine himself a woman after all. Surprised and warmed, she saw what it was that had always been lacking before. Choice. She had never felt free to decide. Sometimes she'd felt obliged. 'We've been going out together for a month now. How much longer must we wait?' Or guilty. 'You don't know what you're doing to me.' Or just plain old-fashioned. 'Everyone does it unless they're frigid.' But she'd never wanted to make love because she felt sorry for someone, or because it was fashionable or she owed it in return for a set number of dinners. She wanted to make love because it felt right and the man was right and she wanted to do it and for no other reason. And here in this dismal place was that most elusive creature. A sexy, fabulous man she liked, who was being honest with her. A man who could take 'no' for an answer. A great warmth enveloped her. She let the torch travel around a bit, admiring his shoulders and the back of his head then all the lovely lines of his back again, down to his behind. Really, he was superb. She glowed with feeling for him.

'That's very fair-minded of you,' she said huskily.

'I'm a fool to myself,' he mocked. 'Stop sweeping that torch over me. I feel like a sex object.'

'What if I said——' She paused, as short on breath as if she was about to climb a sheer cliff without a safety rope. 'That I feel I *could* say no, but I don't want to.'

Sam stopped, hands on hips, and turned to her. 'Is that an invitation, Charlie?' he said softly.

She swallowed hard but could not moisten her dry throat.

'I think it is, Sam,' she croaked. Sam. Love.

A silence stretched out. 'It wouldn't be the way you'd imagined your first time. No moonlight and roses.' He gestured at the canvas bunk. 'No four-poster bed draped in silk.'

'I never really felt moonlight and roses were absolutely necessary,' she said feeling a mild panic set in. What had she done, what had she set in motion? All her ingrained notions of caution and responsibility rose up in outrage.

'I wonder. There's a very romantic streak under that practical surface.' His eyes narrowed. 'I could make you pregnant,' he said flatly.

'I—wouldn't normally take the risk,' she said at last, 'I don't suppose you have anything to—er——' He gave her a quizzical look. 'No, of course you wouldn't have. We might never get out of here so maybe you think it's silly to be talking about—um—consequences,' she said, flushing.

'It's never silly. Only fools rush in.' He smiled. 'What was it your cousin said—''You never take risks with your health''?' He sobered and looked moodily over at her. 'We can—minimise the risk of a child, Charlie, and that's the only risk you'd be taking, you get what I'm saying? I never cheated on my marriage and for once you can believe the papers when they say my name's been linked with that of several women. That's all that was linked—the names,' he said drily. 'I just haven't been in the mood.'

Charlotte stared. All those beautiful girls. 'You mean you haven't had a lover since your divorce?'

Sam blinked. His brows came down in a frown and Charlotte wished she hadn't mentioned the touchy subject of his divorce. She was under no illusion that Sam was in love with her but she certainly didn't want to reinstate the image of his ex-wife right now.

'No,' Sam said at last.

Silence fell again. An owl hooted in a world that might have been a million miles out of reach. The rain had stopped but water still dripped down through the debris.

'If you've changed your mind, tell me now,' he said, on an oddly rough note. 'Before I touch you.'

The words were as evocative as a physical touch. Her nerves leapt, her skin tingled. 'I haven't changed my mind.'

'Then come and dance with me.'

'You said there was no music.'

'I'm hearing something,' he said, smiling. 'Put out the light, Charlie, and come here.'

When she switched out the beam, she held the image of him, eyes half-smiling, half-smouldering, his arms outstretched to her. She didn't even stumble but went straight to him. Amazing, how she could find him in the dark and her with no sense of direction at all.

They danced to no music, scarcely moving. Tentatively, she explored the marvellous curves and planes of his back, let her fingers push into his hair. Sam kissed her and she kissed Sam, question and answer, a tender familiarisation that she wanted to last for hours. Yet, incredibly, she grew dissatisfied. The same languorous quality marked the way he touched her body, holding her, fondling as she pressed close, suddenly impatient with his delicate touch. 'Take it easy, Charlie, darling,' he said and curved his hands over her behind, tilting her wickedly against him. He laughed at her quick indrawn breath.

'I should never have chased you away from my camp,' he said, 'I should have offered you some coffee, invited you in for a swim...we could have made love in the creek——'

'In the creek!'

'Can't swim? All right, then, on the grass in the shade with those pink flowers falling on us.' He unbuttoned her shirt, took it off. 'And I'd dress you in flowers.' He turned her around and unhooked the bra, peeled it off caressingly. 'I'd put one here.' Light as petals dropping, his fingers brushed one breast then the other, 'And here.' Her knees went weak and Charlotte leaned back against him as he caressed her hips, delicately stroked downwards between her thighs. 'And here.' Her senses clamoured, frightening her and she backtracked quickly, taking refuge in words.

'Lady Chatterley,' she said, breathlessly.

'Never met her.'

'*Lady Chatterley's Lover.*'

'Nor him,' said Sam, nuzzling her neck, doing amazing things with his hands. Her voice came out on a gasp.

'It's the flower scene from *Lady Chatterley's Lover.*'

'Trust an English teacher to accuse me of plagiarism at a time like this,' Sam said. 'Be quiet. I haven't finished with the flowers yet...'

She had always thought she'd known what desire was and resisted it, but now she knew she never had. Never this intensity, this leaping response to the merest touch, this primitive need that was an ache inside her. 'Please, Sam——' she whispered, and he picked her up and lay her on the bed while he shed his clothes. His head brushed the hanging copper discs before he stretched out beside her. All the beautiful sculptured bone and muscle of him imprinted on her skin and the chimes rang out a carillon of wild celebration.

'Relax, angel,' he whispered as she tensed, momentarily afraid and vulnerable as he raised himself above her. Suddenly he seemed alien, a powerful force she had unleashed.

Apprehensively she said, 'Sam——'

'We'll stop right now if that's what you want,' he said and like magic, the moment passed. A man who could take no for an answer. She trusted him. With a small laugh of exultation she held him, urged him to her. '*Sam*!' She felt some pain, enough to make her cry out, then Sam was still for a time, stroking her face, letting her grow accustomed to him.

'Oh, Sam,' she breathed. 'It's lovely.'

He laughed and it was lovelier still. Charlotte rocked her hips experimentally. Sam groaned. 'Charlie, take it easy——' Her excitement spiralled and when he moved at last she matched his rhythm, eager for the final discovery.

'You're disappointed,' Sam said, later.

'No, no,' she denied.

He laughed. 'Liar. It would have been better had I not been so nervous.'

Charlotte stirred in the semi-circle of his arm. '*You* were nervous?'

'Well—I've never been a girl's first lover before.'

'Oh.' Some comment appeared to be necessary. 'Well, you were very—er——'

He shook with laughter and she began to feel rather irritated with all this mirth. All very well for *him*, but she felt edgy and vaguely unsatisfied and yes, if she was honest, disappointed.

'Sometimes it isn't much good the first time,' he said.

'The first time I've made love,' she said half to herself. Reality reasserted itself and depression swept over her.

'The first time,' Sam said, folding her over on top of him and arranging her there so promisingly that he hardly had to add, 'But not the last.'

Later. 'So?' he prompted, laughter in his voice, for he already knew. The cellar had echoed with the sounds of her pleasure. His back bore the imprint of her fingernails.

'I—I——' she stammered.

'At last. I've found a way to stop you talking.'

Wrapped in Sam's arms, Charlotte was dreamy, triumphant. She'd scaled the sheer cliff without safety ropes and felt wonderful, daring and free. But the cellar gradually grew chilly again and the sense of freedom vanished. The slide was more desolate now, from euphoria down into the quicksand.

'There's this dress I saw last week in a boutique,' she announced loudly. *Stamp out quicksand*. 'A ridiculous dress. Strapless, slinky, black. The boutique has potted kumquat trees each side of its doors and no prices on the window displays so it would undoubtedly cost the earth.'

'Undoubtedly,' Sam murmured.

'I probably wouldn't get to wear a dress like that more than twice, so it would be grossly impractical to buy it.'

'Grossly impractical.'

'I never wear black. Everyone says black doesn't suit me. And I'm not the strapless, slinky type, am I?'

'No comment. The army boots are clouding my judgement.'

'If—*when* I get out of here,' she said fiercely, making a vow of it to save herself from the quicksand, 'I'm going to *buy* that dress.'

Sam's laughter boomed around the rafters. 'I bet you won't, Charlie. Once outside again you'll go all sensible and talk yourself out of it.'

'How much do you bet?'

'Twenty bucks.'

They shook hands on it. 'What else will you do when you're outside again?' Sam asked.

'Write my book. Travel. Start a really large quilting project.' Then darkly, she added, 'Take a course in orienteering so I don't lose my way again. You?'

'Ah. I'll be nice to the Press, get myself re-instated as a father, write to my mother and—make time to coach some junior players.'

'Tell me about playing cricket,' she said, snuggling in.

He chuckled. 'It was that good, huh?'

'I don't know what you mean.'

'Angel, you gave me to understand that listening to cricket stories was a fate worse than death. The afterglow must be really something.'

'It is, but it's wearing off, so tell me how you got to be such a big shot in cricket before it's gone and I regain my senses.'

So he told her. The early successes, the boy out of school catapulted into a man's sport, into the public eye. The first long walk across the green at Lords with television cameras zooming in and commentators predicting that a temperamental twenty-year-old didn't have the match experience to perform. Dejection when they were proved right. Later, the savage pleasure of proving them wrong. Pre-match nerves, frustration, injuries. Adulation and unanswerable criticism. Above it all, playing the game, loving it. Wanting a place in its history with the other great players whose names he quoted as if they were contemporaries. Charlotte was surprised to find that Sam's heroes lived and played the game fifty, seventy, a hundred years ago. For millions they lived on in a sport with a history as powerful and immediate as that of any country.

'I stayed too long.' The admission came stiffly from him as if it had cost him to say it. 'It all started to go wrong but I thought I could turn it around. I wanted to go out in a blaze of glory.'

Sam was silent for a long time and she wondered if he was deciding to cut his losses or to stay in there, trying for one more burst of glory before he retired. Perhaps he was hooked, and even a soured stardom was better than none. Sam's grand passion. Marriage would have been a strain—one grand passion too many.

At last he stirred, nuzzled in to her. 'How's the afterglow?'

'Gone,' she said mournfully.

'Well,' he said, 'If I want to tell you about my best season we'll have to organise some afterglow.'

Her body shook off its drowsiness, zinged with life. 'But—I mean, *again*?' she said, impressed. 'Haven't I read that athletes can have a lot of troubles with—er—that kind of thing?'

'You're underestimating the sportsman's urge.'

Charlotte, clasped to him, thigh to thigh, gulped. 'I don't think I am.'

Sam's smirk was in his voice. 'I mean the sportsman's urge to talk about his matches. I'm only doing this to put you in the mood for the Test Series against the West Indies, summer of——'

Charlotte groaned and shortly afterwards groaned again and some time after that she went out on a blaze of glory.

CHAPTER SIX

THE sound of a voice woke them in the morning. A man's voice.

'Funny,' it said faintly somewhere above. 'That bike out the front—someone must be here. I reckon it's Sam Buchanan.'

'Wishful thinking, mate,' a second man said. 'We won't get to meet him, couldn't be that lucky. 'Struth. The roof's gone, look at that.'

Charlotte and Sam looked at each other, slow to believe what they were hearing. In unison they shot up.

'Here! Down here!' Sam bellowed.

'What was that?' the first man said. 'Sounded like a voice.'

'Nah. Crows.'

Charlotte jangled the wind chimes. Sam bellowed through the length of pipe. There was a short, startled silence, then, much closer, the first man's voice. 'G'day. That you down there, Mr Buchanan?'

'Yes, in the cellar,' Sam called.

''Struth!' said the second man.

'There, see—Sam Buchanan! Told you!' The first man was triumphant. 'We'll get you out, Mr Buchanan, no worries. We're the Marshall Brothers, Demolition Specialists, Mr Buchanan. Ross and Barry. Happened to be in the district and called in to have a look at the place so we could give you that quote you wanted. Reckon you started without us,' he said laconically. A pause. 'Nice to meet you Mr Buchanan. Reckon this is our lucky day.'

They went away to alert the authorities. Charlotte giggled and cried. '*Their* lucky day.'

'The wreckers—how does that symbolism strike you, Charlie?' Sam said, hugging her. 'Saved by the wreckers!'

Eventually the police came, and the emergency rescue squad and the Marshall brothers with a crane and lifting equipment, and, of course, the Press. One enterprising photographer must have stretched flat on the ground to aim his camera through an air vent. The blue-white light blinded Sam and Charlotte. Sam cursed, and even when the eager cameraman had been removed by police he remained wary and thoughtful.

'Angel, we'd better get a few things straight.'

Charlotte snuggled up against him, smiling dreamily now that freedom was so close. 'What things, Sam?'

'The Press are going to blow this up out of proportion if we're not careful. For both our sakes, let's keep this episode as uncomplicated as possible. The story is, we're just two strangers who happened to get stranded together, OK?'

Charlotte picked up on the key words. Uncomplicated. Strangers. Sam shifted, putting a small space between them.

'If you go out there with that starry-eyed look, people might get the wrong idea,' he went on, putting even more space between them.

'The wrong idea?' she said.

'They might think there's something—between us,' he said harshly.

And there isn't. That's what he was telling her. The unspoken words echoed around the cellar. Charlotte was shaken out of the false little world she was in. The prospect of freedom had come as a bonus to the wonderful new feelings she had for Sam. In her euphoria and shock, she hadn't realised that it was a direct trade. Sam went with the cellar. Not with freedom. She couldn't have both. But she would have come to the realisation in time, she thought, feeling a draught of cold air as the rescuers shifted something. She would have come to it reluctantly, unlike Sam who wasn't wasting any time detaching himself from a lover who might cling. She was angry with herself for being taken by surprise. After all, Sam had made no promises. In fact he'd made it crystal-clear that he wanted no involvement. It hadn't seemed to matter when they were taking one day at a time. Pride demanded a positive response. She laughed.

'Relax, Sam. I wasn't planning on continuing our *episode*. You won't have to change your phone number, or warn your secretary about me. I promise,' she added on a ragged note of flippancy, 'not to lurk naked in hotel rooms.'

He snorted. 'Charlie, that wasn't what I——'

'Sam, it's all right. I'm aware that in the normal way of things you and I wouldn't get together in a million years. It was nice but it's over.'

He frowned at that. Charlotte felt some savage satisfaction. Maybe he'd expected tears and recriminations. But she had to be fair. Sam had been honest with her, told her no lies, used no male trickery to get what he wanted. He had proved to her that a special kind of man did exist and she was grateful. 'But I want you to know—that I'll always remember you as very special.' Her voice wobbled. Sam didn't appear thrilled by the idea of a permanent place in her memory.

Soon, she thought dismally, she might deteriorate into tears if not recriminations. She jumped up, fighting the feeling and grabbed the pen from her backpack. Vigorously, she attacked the graffiti.

'What are you doing? Leaving your mark with a message? Charlotte was here?' he asked in a rough voice.

Stamp out quicksand. Forget the notes and play the music. Hummingbirds have forgotten the words. Love rules.

'No,' she said, slashing a line through 'forgotton'. 'Before I go I just have to correct the spelling.'

The rescuers and the wreckers wanted to know what Sam was laughing about.

* * *

As a rescue it was more like a circus. The emergency
crew bellowed orders, police relayed messages on radios
and the media flashed lights and microphones. The
Marshall brothers shouted down details of the progress
in between reminiscences of a match against the West
Indies in which Sam took six wickets from some of the
world's most spectacular and athletic batsmen.
'Brisbane, at the Gabba,' Barry said. 'We used to do a
lot of work in Brisbane.' There was something surreal-
istic about the serious discussion of the fall of wickets
on a fine Sunday afternoon four years ago, while machinery crashed and dust flew. And there was something
steadying about it too. It was a tale of struggle, of noble
individual efforts and valiant team work, every detail
remembered and recounted. They went on to discuss
another match played eighty years ago, never seen by
any of them but recounted by grandfathers and fathers.
Like the songs of medieval troubadors, cricket stories
passed down through time, Charlotte thought, and found
it oddly comforting.

It was dusk when Sam and Charlotte were freed at
last and Cranston was a mess. Other internal walls had
fallen, their rubble pushed aside in heaps to make way
for the rescue team. Electrical cord, carrying bare light
bulbs, festooned the remaining walls, and the effect was
oddly festive, as if Cranston were expecting guests for
a ball. Framed in each of the arched, empty doorways
was a vignette of the sunset sky, apricot and indigo, with
hills and trees silhouetted against it. To Charlotte, accustomed to days of near darkness, the fading light
seemed brilliant. The air was cool and smelled of euca-
lyptus and grass and petrol fumes. Down by the creek,
a kookaburra laughed.

Swathed in a blanket, she drank some hot tea someone
gave her. There were no familiar faces in the crowd.
Charlotte wondered who she was hoping to see. Her
parents? She smiled wryly at the idea. Grahame Norris
had turned up, beaming from ear to ear.

'Couldn't be better,' she heard him say, *sotto voce* to Sam. 'This is just what you needed to get some good Press.'

Sam, squinting at Cranston's upper storey, sighed. 'For pity's sake, Grahame. I couldn't give a——'

'Hey. Don't knock it,' Grahame said. 'Champions could use a little positive publicity and it wouldn't do your custody case any harm either to look the hero, you get what I'm saying?'

Sam snapped to attention at that and he remained thoughtful as the helpers milled around, shutting down the rescue operation.

'So, where's the girl?' Grahame asked, a creative gleam in his eye.

Absently Sam introduced her. Grahame looked her over as if he was auditioning her for the part of Sam's sidekick in this little drama. Teeth on edge, stung by Sam's distant manner, she felt like shouting at him, this is real. I am a real, live person. It was a moment or two before he recognised her.

'Well, well,' he said speculatively. 'You told me you'd get to see him one way or another. How did you track him down?'

'Oh, sheer luck,' said Charlotte ironically.

They were taken to the nearest hospital where Charlotte's various cuts were swabbed with antiseptic and Sam's leg was examined and strapped. Charlotte emerged into the soulless casualty waiting-room to see Sam, hands on hips, talking to the Marshall brothers who had annexed him as their own special property. His attention shifted sharply from Grahame as footsteps pattered along the corridor and a high, treble voice shrieked, 'Daddy! Daddy!'

A small boy tore across the open space and Sam, his reflexes slow for once, stood frozen. Then he bent and clumsily swept the child into his arms.

'Stevie——' His voice cracked. As he clasped his son, there was a look on his face so raw that Charlotte averted her eyes to give him that moment in privacy.

'You're the girlfriend, I take it,' a voice drawled beside Charlotte. Startled, she turned to see a tall woman in red. She was beautiful. Matt, perfect skin and straight, dark hair that hung like a fall of silk to her shoulders. Her eyes were an incredible tigerish bronze. This had to be Stevie's mother. Sam's ex-wife. Ruth.

Ruth struck a pose, one slender hand raised, the wrist thrown back. Her frosted nails glittered; the smoke from her cigarette caught at Charlotte's dusty throat, made her cough. She stood there spluttering, a dusty, ragged scarecrow beside Sam's beautiful, glamorous ex-wife. Weary and suffering post-rescue depression, Charlotte was woman enough to be annoyed by the contrast. She just managed to hold back the futile gesture of smoothing her hair.

'A rough break for you,' Ruth said. She looked Charlotte over as if assessing how well she might scrub up. 'You're not one of the model types he's been seeing,' she commented. It didn't seem to please her much. 'Not very discreet of you, getting sprung like that. Away for the weekend in the country together, were you—and the roof fell in?' She quirked a brow, glanced over at Sam. 'It isn't enough for Sam just to make the earth move.' She smiled glacially at her own witticism.

Charlotte flushed. She felt awkward and defensive with this woman who had shared Sam's life, borne his child. And somehow, unfairly, she felt second-best. 'No—it wasn't—it was sheer coincidence——' she began, when Grahame came hurrying over with the guarded look of an umpire.

'Ruth,' he said with his toothy smile. 'We didn't expect to see you here. Should you be smoking in a hospital, darling?'

She paid no attention to the dry endearment nor to the criticism. 'Stevie saw a news flash on the television and I had to bring him to prove his father was safe,' she said, watching Sam and Stevie through narrowed eyes. 'I'll be taking him home again in a few minutes. I don't want him mixed up with that Press rabble waiting out there.'

Grahame was visibly relieved at the news that she wasn't staying.

'Find me an ashtray, will you, Grahame, darling,' Ruth said in the assured tone of a woman for whom men jumped through hoops. She waved her cigarette with a half-inch of ash ready to fall and Grahame went to oblige. When he'd gone, she turned to Charlotte, smiling faintly. 'Sam's a very attractive man. Also very rich. But if it's his money you've got your eye on, pet, think again. I have first claim and a very good lawyer. He'll only be half as rich by the time I've finished divorcing him.'

Grahame came back, offering a cheap glass saucer. Without looking at him, Ruth stubbed the cigarette out and left him standing like a servant with the used ashtray. As she went to claim Stevie from Sam, the light flashed from the diamond rings she wore with her plain gold wedding-band.

By the time I've finished divorcing him...

Charlotte felt light-headed. Sam was still married. She remembered now that he'd never actually said he was divorced. He'd said his marriage was over and his wedding-ring was out of date but he couldn't get it off and she had assumed there had been a divorce. And he'd let her assume.

There was a stiff little exchange between Sam and Ruth, the child hugged his father one last time. Sam walked along behind Ruth and Stevie as if prolonging the moment of parting and Grahame dashed around, guiding them to an exit safe from the Press rabble.

He'd had a perfect opportunity to tell her. 'You haven't had a lover since your divorce?' she'd said, that night just before they'd danced in the dark. He should have

told her then that there'd been no divorce, but he hadn't.
Her face flamed.

Sam came back, indefinably straighter and stronger.
He came over to her and smiled. 'I've been thinking
about Cranston——' he began.

Charlotte looked coldly at him and said, 'I see your
wife can't get *her* wedding ring off, either.'

Involuntarily, Sam looked at his left hand.
'Charlie——'

She dodged past him and ran, not caring where and
blundered into a huddle of photographers. Grahame
caught her up before she could say anything in answer
to their questions. 'OK, folks,' he said jovially, putting
a protective arm around Charlotte. 'Give the poor kid
a chance. Wait till Sam gets here.' To Charlotte he said,
as he led her into a room bristling with microphones and
cameras, 'Might as well get it over with now, love. It's
Sam they want, so keep it simple. Just look exhausted
and give a wan smile now and then. We'll cover for you,
OK?'

Sam arrived a moment later, limping slightly, the
strapping on his leg visible through his ripped, frayed
jeans. Unshaven and wearing an expression of becoming
modesty, he looked, she thought sourly, like Indiana
Jones returning from his latest adventure. Every lens in
the place turned to him.

'Are you glad to be out of there?' 'How do you feel?'
'Were you worried?' Sam treated the babble of inane
questions with good humour. He positively vibrated with
strength and purpose, holding their attention so com-
pletely that Charlotte might as well have been invisible.
She couldn't keep her eyes off him, either. Sam seemed
to have taken new life from the past few days. He was
renewed, revived. 'We all need the kiss of life from time
to time, to revive us...'

The whole thing had been a kiss of life to Sam, just
what he'd needed. Adventure, the invigorating threat to

existence, even a woman to fall in love with him for the duration. A hero's welcome from his son.

She, on the other hand, had lost a tripod and damaged a camera, she thought sourly. And that was only for starters. The last of her energy seemed to slip away as she sat there, excluded even in the spotlight. It was an old, familiar feeling.

Inevitably, though, she was asked questions, and as Grahame had promised he and Sam covered for her so efficiently that she never managed to make a reply.

'Naturally she was scared to death. Lucky Sam was there, eh, love?' Grahame said, busy putting Sam back on his pedestal and conveniently ignoring the fact that if Sam hadn't been there there wouldn't have been any accident.

Didn't anyone use proper names any more? 'Angel' from Sam. 'Pet' from his wife. 'Love' from his manager. My name is Charlotte.

'Why were you out there, Miss Wells?' a reporter asked.

'She's a keen amateur photographer,' Sam said with a smile that would have turned her efforts into the tinkering of a kid with a box Brownie had she not been wearing the bulky Chinon around her neck. Charlotte experienced another mild bout of irritation. 'Luckily she took a picnic lunch with her, so we had something to eat. What was in those sandwiches, angel?'

'Cheese and pickle.' She stared fixedly at Sam. Her image was being shaped for the media by him and Grahame. Poor little kid with a camera and a picnic basket, comforted and protected by the big hero. Sam didn't seem to want her to say why she'd been at Cranston. Something bothered her about that more than anything else. Tiredly she grappled with it and almost missed it. Of course. Cranston. Her eyes widened. Sam wanted to wreck Cranston and it wasn't in his interest to let her talk about photographing its heritage value.

For just a split second she didn't care, could have closed
her eyes and let him get away with it.

But she heard herself saying, 'No matter what, Sam,
I want you to know that you'll always be special to me.'
She went over the naïve statement in her mind, viciously,
furiously, hating herself for her easy belief. He'd been
special because he hadn't used any cheap tricks, she
thought. Gallant Sam Buchanan had given her that rare
chance to choose, she thought. The man who could take
no for an answer. He made certain he wouldn't have to
take no for an answer by not telling her the truth because it might have spoiled his chances of getting her
into bed. It enraged her. It hurt and humiliated her that
Sam had shrewdly seen the ideals she'd clung to and used
them against her.

'OK, angel?' he said in a low voice, leaning towards
her with avuncular concern.

She looked into those blue eyes and hated him. How
convenient for Sam if she tamely went along with this
little act. Good old Charlotte who didn't cling when the
affair was over, didn't make waves about his house-
wrecking plans. In a day or two he could almost forget
she'd ever existed. Charlotte who? She discovered a
sudden yearning to make waves. An unexpected surge
of energy straightened her in her chair.

'I was at the house taking photographs,' she said
clearly. 'For the Heritage and History Society. We've
petitioned Mr Buchanan to delay bringing in the
wreckers.'

The Marshall brothers looked hurt by this and Sam
sent her a narrow look, but he needn't have been worried.
There was minimal interest in Charlotte's revelation. She
was only a minor player; the house had collapsed after
all, and there were enough stories around with a con-
servation slant. The attention went back to Sam and the
interview came to a halt. As Grahame got into his
sheepdog act, herding them out, a reporter said to

Charlotte, 'What was your name again?' and she said
clearly,

'Charlotte Wells—Wells as in Martin and Linda.'

'Of Earthbound?' he said, alert now.

'My parents.'

Now that *did* interest them. As Earthbound's daughter
her petition to Sam Buchanan was suddenly back on the
agenda. Grahame said plaintively, 'Why didn't I know
about this?' Sam stared at her.

The room was almost cleared but there were a couple
of Press people left to pick up this story bonus. Would
Miss Wells actually agitate for the preservation of a
building so unstable that its roof collapsed on her? Miss
Wells said she would. What did Mr Buchanan have to
say to that? Mr Buchanan managed a laugh and a tolerant comment about the emotional strain Miss Wells
was under, but Charlotte knew he was furious.

At this point Grahame rounded up the stragglers and
headed them out. Sam turned a thunderous look on
Charlotte.

'Quite a little bombshell you dropped there, angel.
How come I didn't get to hear about Mom and Pop and
the Top Forty when you were baring your soul in the
cellar?'

'You didn't tell me everything, either,' she pointed out.

Sam's eyes narrowed on her. She recognised that look.
A re-assessment of her, based on her parentage. She'd
liked being just Charlotte to Sam, not Martin and Linda
Wells's daughter. And wasn't that ironic? The only time
in her life she'd ever hogged the limelight and she'd had
to use her parents to do it.

'What the *hell* did you do it for?'

'Maybe I didn't want my only Press quote to read
"Cheese and pickle",' she snapped. 'You were trying to
gag me, you and your sheepdog. And, what's worse,
you were making me look a complete idiot while you
were playing the big hero.'

'We were trying to protect you. Ease you out of the picture so you could keep your privacy.'

'Afterwards you would have gone on ignoring our petition and our letters——'

'You know that for a fact, do you?' he said harshly.

'Whereas, now that it's a matter of public record that you own Cranston, you'll have to be more careful.'

His jaw jutted. 'You think so?'

Charlotte leaned pugnaciously towards him. 'It wouldn't be good for your image to knock down a lovely old heritage building just like that!' She clicked her fingers in his face and Sam mashed his lips together. 'You'd never get back on your pedestal doing things like that. Ask Grahame.'

'If you imagine that you've backed me into a corner with this—little piece of melodrama tonight, you're very much mistaken.' He took her arm in an iron grip and thrust his face close to hers. 'Don't start congratulating yourself, angel. You haven't forced me into anything. I'll do what I want with my own property, do you understand me?' He gave her a shake and without warning, all the stiffening went out of her. She staggered and Sam put his arm around her waist and she found herself leaning on him, her cheek resting on his shoulder. She had a temporary memory lapse and put her arms around him, closed her eyes. It was all right now. She could rely on Sam. The treacherous lapse passed and she drew back.

'You're out on your feet,' he said curtly, taking her towards the door. The corridor was empty apart from a nurse with a trolley and a hurrying figure in the distance. 'The police put your car in the hospital car park. Is anyone here to take you home? Your parents?' He looked down at her, frowning. 'No, I suppose not.'

It was almost too much for Charlotte. She stifled a hysterical giggle. Sam was a rat but his instinct to protect transcended even his fury at being thwarted. Maybe he *had* been trying to protect her from the Press earlier. It confused her.

'My cousin. Gale,' she said, indicating the distant figure, now running. Grahame came and hustled Sam away, followed closely by the Marshall brothers expressing their concern that his strained leg muscle might delay his return to form. Gale rushed, arms outspread to hug Charlotte.

'Charls—you're OK! I couldn't believe it when they phoned me. I tried to ring Auntie Linda and Uncle Martin but they're in Adelaide at some music festival.'

'Doesn't matter,' Charlotte said dully, stifling a sharp, childish wish for the parents who were always somewhere else.

'I'm sorry, so *sorry*.' Gale wept over Charlotte's shoulder. 'It was rotten and I shouldn't have done it and I promise you, really *promise*, it won't ever happen again.'

'Gale—what are you talking about?'

'Your *jeans*!' she cried in anguish. 'I took your jeans and then you didn't come home and you could have died in that place and your last thought about me would have been that I was rotten enough to take your Levis!'

The hysterical desire to laugh grew stronger. 'When my life was flashing before my eyes, I didn't think about my jeans, believe me. Let's go home. Did you bring your car? We'll collect mine tomorrow.'

She looked back but Sam had gone. A stray reporter caught her as she was leaving. 'You must feel very lucky, Miss Wells?' He seemed to expect an answer to the idiotic question.

'Oh, I do,' she said gravely.

She felt a bit light-headed as Gale drove them home. Her cousin was making all kinds of resolutions.

'And I'm going to keep my washing and ironing up to date and I'm *never* going to borrow your things again,' she declared. 'And from now on I'm going to be more careful. I mean, if something like this can happen to *you*, I've been living on borrowed time. Of course, it wasn't entirely horrible, I suppose—I mean, you could have been buried alive with a creep instead of Sam Buchanan.' She left a hopeful little space in case Charlotte felt like filling in details about Sam but when she didn't, went on. 'Oh, Charls, I didn't have a clue where you were and I would have if I'd listened to you. I'm going to be a good listener from now on. Are you all right?' she asked as Charlotte gave a hiccup of laughter.

'*Lucky*, the man said.' It might take some time to sort out how lucky she felt. It had been a revelation. A lifetime lived out in a few days. She had discovered real fear and faced her own mortality, discovered things about herself that she might not have known otherwise. That she had more courage than she knew, that she had a wild side, a passionate side. And was that good, or bad to know that? She laughed.

Gale glanced anxiously at her. 'Don't, Charls. It gives me the creeps when you laugh like that.'

Charlotte couldn't stop laughing. 'I still don't know, isn't that a scream?' she said, 'I can't decide.'

'Decide what?'

Without warning, the laughter went. She leaned back and stared through the windscreen at an incomparable sky full of cloud and stars. 'Whether thirteen is my lucky or unlucky number.'

CHAPTER SEVEN

THE photocopier hummed through fifty copies of a quiz on the Brontës. Charlotte stood there watching the sheets slide through without really seeing them. Most of the students and teaching staff had gone home and the school had settled into its Wednesday after-hours life. Trombones and trumpets sounded intermittently as the brass band practised in the school hall. Whistles shrilled on the netball courts and from the sports field came the sharp crack of cricket ball on bat and the shouts of the coach. The school year was now in its fourth and final term after two weeks of holidays. It was a month since the rescue from Cranston.

Her parents had come back from Adelaide, to find that the record producer who had masterminded their Australian releases had disappeared into the blue with his trumpet and a suspected nervous breakdown. Genuine friendship for the man, and a superstitious reluctance to continue with the new album without him, set them off on an immediate search. They managed to phone Charlotte in between their enquiries and frantic rearrangements of schedules. Their concern, horror and relief at her ordeal was tempered with surprise that she'd shared it with someone almost as famous as themselves and it was all condensed into one burst of attention making up in intensity for what it lacked in duration.

'You're safe, that's what matters,' her mother said on a final note before she moved on to more current events. 'It looks as if Sid has headed west. He could be in a pub anywhere between here and Bourke. We could be weeks finding him.'

As Sid, aged forty-nine, wore pastel trousers, bleached his hair and favoured a single ruby ear-stud, Charlotte had a feeling he might be noticed in the outback rather sooner than later. Charlotte passed on the hummingbird graffito to her father who said, vaguely, 'Oh, yes, that's nice.'

At school, the students had created a whole new range of jokes about Miss Wells's captivity with a millionaire sportsman, concentrating on puns about cricket balls and maiden overs. Once she found a chalked message waiting for her on a blackboard before a sniggering class eager for her reaction. 'What did you do in the celler, Miss Wells?' She viewed it dispassionately, circled 'celler' and said, as she vigorously re-wrote the word, 'Cellar is spelled with an "a".' She'd never been more pleased to find a spelling mistake.

As she'd predicted, she'd gone back to square one with Christopher Dunlop, who had reverted to uninterested shrugs. Women's magazines pestered her for the story of her captivity with Sam, and Brian seemed as annoyed by it as if she'd done it on purpose.

'I feel a bit of a laughing stock, if you must know,' he'd said seriously when she'd asked him point-blank if something was bothering him. 'It was common knowledge that I was taking you out. How do you think I feel now that everyone's talking about you spending the weekend with Sam Buchanan?'

'Spending the weekend?' She flushed, remembering Ruth Buchanan implying something similar. 'I didn't know the man from Adam.' A very appropriate comparison, considering the Eden-like setting and Sam's lack of a fig leaf. The thought deepened her flush. 'Are you suggesting I had an assignation with him? Do I *look* the type to hotfoot off to the country to—to swim nude in the creek and share a tent with a bad-tempered millionaire sportsman who plays *cricket*, the most boring sport ever created?'

Brian was puzzled by the introduction of nude swimming but pleased with the description of Sam. 'You won't be seeing Buchanan again?'

'Why would I?' she said, giving a shrug worthy of
Christopher Dunlop.

'Well—he's a celebrity, and you mix with a lot of
them.'

Brian spoke as if celebrities were a breed apart. It was
one of the things she liked about Brian. Unlike other
people she knew, he never pestered for an introduction
to her parents, or free tickets to a rock concert, or an
invitation to a celebrity party. 'That is one very good
reason not to see him again.' Not, she thought, that she
would feel any need to explain to Brian if she did.

But in spite of her irritation with him, when Brian
asked her to dinner and a film she said yes. The sooner
she got back to ordinary life the better. Now, as she
watched the last copy of the Brontë quiz slide through,
she thought guiltily that Brian might not like to be tagged
'ordinary life'.

She inserted the copies in her folder for the next day,
collected a pile of assignments to work on at home and
slipped a book into her bag. It was a second-hand copy
of a book about bridges she had bought for Christopher.
He hadn't been at school this past week but she kept
bringing the book hoping to give it to him.

Her car was one of the last in the car park and there
wasn't a student in sight. Just as well. Because a black
BMW was parked near the gate and the man talking on
the car phone in the passenger seat would have had kids
clamouring for autographs. Grahame was at the wheel,
fingers tapping on the dashboard, eyes flicking between
the rear-view and side mirrors. The picture of a man
about to make a run for it. He opened the door and
looked at her assessingly. Because she'd put pressure on
his boss over Cranston—or because of her parentage?

'Recovered now?' he asked to her surprise.

'Fine.' She tried to keep her eyes off Sam, who was
still on the phone. 'What are you doing here?'

Grahame glanced at Sam, speculatively again at
Charlotte.

'If you don't know, pet—I'm damned sure I don't.'

Sam saw her, put down the phone and, with a few words to Grahame, got out and came around the car, examining every detail of her appearance on the way.

'I hate your hair like that. It makes you look like a schoolmarm stereotype,' Sam said, stopping an arm's length away. Considering the length of his arms, it was a fair distance, but still too close. Sam, in a three-piece suit cut by a master hand. Sam in a collar and silk tie, his jaw smooth-shaven, his hair trimmed and brushed and glossy in the sunlight. She'd seen him in shades of grey and dust and had almost forgotten how startling he looked in colour. Tan skin and hair the colour of mahogany, eyes a startling blue.

'You haven't re-grown that stupid moustache, I see,' she said in self-defence, and felt a stab of childish satisfaction when he raised his hand involuntarily to his mouth. Aware of Grahame watching, she turned away and hurried to her car. 'Go away, Sam. I've had enough notoriety. If the boys in the cricket team come up from the oval and find you here, I'll never hear the end of it.'

'If you didn't want notoriety you should have kept quiet at the news conference,' he said, taking the keys from her as she attempted to re-align her load. 'And if you don't want any more, you'll get in the car and drive me home before someone gets a picture of us together.'

'Surely photographers aren't still chasing you?'

Sam quirked a brow as if to say, Why not? I'm still God's gift to the camera.

Alarmed, she glanced around then got in the car in case he was correct. Sam took her keys and let himself in on the passenger side.

'What do you mean—drive you home?' she said, catching the keys he tossed to her. 'There's your car——' Even as she said it the BMW wheeled around, kicked up dust and bounded on to the road. Grahame drove the same way he did everything else.

'I want to talk to you. Turn right when you get to the main road,' Sam said, looking at her books and folders one by one as he transferred them to the back seat.

'All right. Talk to me. Then I'll drop you at the nearest cab rank.'

'You going to eject me bodily, Charlie?' he said with a maddeningly complacent smile that made her grind her teeth. He held up the last book. *'Famous Bridges of the World*? Let me guess—propaganda for Christopher?'

'I found it at a flea-market and bought it for him, yes,' she said shortly, slotting the key in the ignition.

He leaned around to set the book on her crowded back seat. His attention was caught by the large transparent bag of multi-coloured fabric, the portable sewing machine for her class that night. 'The large quilting project?' he enquired, aggravatingly coming to the right conclusion.

'What do you want to talk about? If it's Cranston, then you've received our petition.'

His genial expression vanished. 'Oh, yes. Let me tell you again that no amount of public screeching about heritage and obligation will make me do anything I don't want.'

Just then, Brian walked out to the car park in company with the head and deputy. He looked over at Charlotte's car and waved before he saw her passenger. The late afternoon sun flashed on the lenses of his glasses. He frowned, seemed undecided for a moment then moved forward a little and called, 'See you at seven tomorrow night, Charlotte.'

Staking his claim, she thought, but gritted her teeth in a smile as he reluctantly decided against interrupting their tête-à-tête. No doubt Brian would feel entitled to a full explanation as to why Sam was here. As Brian drove past, the two men looked hard at each other.

'I take it that's Brian? Where's he taking you tomorrow night?'

She started the car. 'To a movie.'

'A movie! Quilting classes, historical meetings and the
movies with good old Brian. You haven't decided on
anything more exciting, then, having been snatched from
the jaws of death?'

'I don't find Brian dull, if that's what you're implying. He has a lot of fine qualities.'

'Like what?'

'He's pleasant, cultured, highly intelligent. And,' she
added, putting her foot on the accelerator, 'he's *single*.'

It silenced him. If she hadn't a healthy regard for his
resilience she might have thought he was embarrassed.
He gave directions to his place. It was St Leonards, inner
city, all architectural angles and enclosing walls, the only
contemporary building in a street of Edwardian semi-
detached houses.

'Very appropriate,' Charlotte said as she pulled up
outside a gate set into a stone wall.

'What is?'

'I presume an old house had to be knocked down
before this could be built. An ideal site for you.'

Sam's eyes glinted. 'Two old houses, in fact, but they
fell down. Termites. Some old heaps don't need any help
from bulldozers.'

He got out of the car and, puzzled, she said, 'You
haven't said what you wanted to talk about.'

Sam leaned in the open door, studying her thoughtfully. 'Just wanted to see if you were OK, Charlie. Is
everything all right?'

'No, of course it's not all right,' she said irritably.
'I'm sick to death of sly remarks and cricket metaphors
in the classroom, I'm fed up with men looking at me as
if I might be some kind of temptress in disguise. I've
had it up to *here* with a rotten little magazine that keeps
pursuing me for an interview and if Gale asks me one
more time what it's like to wake beside Sam Buchanan
himself——' She stopped, reddened a bit as she caught
Sam's eye, and remembered just what it had been like
to wake beside him.

'Mmm—but, I mean—is everything all right?'

The quiet, insistent note got through to her. 'I'm not pregnant, if that's what you mean, Sam,' she said abruptly.

His relief was no more heartfelt than her own had been, but contrarily it angered her. She had almost begun to think he'd looked her up simply because he wanted to see her, because in some small way he felt the bond that she felt. But Sam only wanted to be sure he had created no new area of responsibility which might involve him.

The gate in the wall opened and a little boy came hurtling through. Sam crouched down, held out his arms and Stevie ran into them and was borne upwards. Charlotte would have driven off immediately but Sam had left the passenger door open. She tried closing it from the inside but her neat, straight skirt didn't allow enough movement so she walked around to close it, drawn by the picture of Sam with his son. With the child, he dropped his shuttered look. There was no caution in him, no holding back, just love, pure and uncomplicated. If ever he loved a woman the way he loved his son, she would go up in flames. Before Charlotte could get back in the car, Sam came over, carrying Stevie. There was the swagger of pride in his walk.

'Say hello to Charlie,' he bade his son.

'I saw you at the hospital,' Stevie said. 'You had a camera around your neck.'

'Did I?' Her recollection was hazy. What else had this observant child noticed?

'Anyway, Charlie's a boy's name,' he said.

'It's short for Charlotte. The way Stevie is short for Steven,' she told him, looking into candid blue eyes very like Sam's might have been before he wearied of everything but his son. She was judged and apparently considered OK, for he said, with an air of conferring a favour, 'I'll show you my new bike—you wait here. Wait.' The little boy scrambled down Sam as if he were

a tree and ran through the gate. Charlotte cursed silently.
She didn't want to get involved with Sam's family scene
but she couldn't bring herself to flatten the ego of a child.

'Stevie's staying with you?' she said.

'For a time. Things are looking up. Mrs Hume's for-
given me the nightclub incident now that I've done
penance in the cellar, and I've called a truce with Ruth.
We've talked at last, come to some agreement over Stevie.
I have you to thank for that, partly.'

'Me?'

'You forced me to remember the old days, the way it
was with us before it all went wrong. We'd forgotten all
that in recriminations. Remembering those times helped
take some of the sting out, talk sensibly for a change.'

Oh, terrific, she thought. Paris in the summer, relived
in the dark. Was there a reunion in the offing? Would
the divorce be postponed indefinitely? And he had *her*
to thank for it! If she tried really hard she could save
Cranston as well. Perhaps she could put together a new
career, saving old homes and restoring families to live
in them. 'Good,' she said, shortly.

The bike sped through the gate towards her, bell
trilling. Dutifully she admired the red enamel finish, the
blue vinyl seat and the training wheels. 'Soon I won't
need those,' he said with four-year-old braggadocio.
'Have you got your camera in the car? 'Cos if you have,
you can take a picture of me on my bike.'

'No. My camera isn't working.'

Sam had the grace to look guilty.

'You can get a new one then come back and take my
picture,' Stevie told her handsomely. 'I'll ring you up,
'cos I know how to use the phone. And I can run fast
too. You can take some pictures of me running fast.'

'Thank you,' she said gravely.

'That's all right.' Stevie was all largesse. 'Watch me
ride fast up the front path.'

She watched him go. Whatever damage Ruth and Sam
had done to each other, their son seemed to be surviving

with his confidence intact. 'Your son is a very nice little boy. Do you ever take him to see the house his family built? Will you take him to watch it being wrecked?'

'Angel, does it ever occur to you that you can oversell a cause?' he said in a weary voice. 'I think the building's dangerous and should come down. But—I'm prepared to listen to some expert opinions.'

She stared. 'That's reasonable,' she said at last, warned by the steely look in his eye not to press her advantage with further argument right now. 'At least it's a stay of execution for a few months.'

'If the old place lasts that long,' he said drily, following her around to close the door as she got into the car. 'I've written to your Mrs Fulbright to call off the dogs—or do I mean cats?'

'You mean the society has received a *letter* from the elusive Sam Buchanan at last?' she said, wide-eyed. 'Things *are* looking up.'

He laughed. 'Be careful with your fellow-teacher, angel. Those quiet, academic types can be unpredictable.' He gave a tigerish growl.

'That's where you're wrong. Brian is not at all unpredict——' She bit her lip, seeing the trap too late.

He leaned on the car window-ledge, grinning. 'I'll bet you haven't bought that black dress yet.'

Charlotte started the car and met his eyes without blinking. 'You lose. You owe me twenty bucks.'

He stepped back sharply as she shot from the kerb. Her haughty departure was spoiled somewhat by the need to return Stevie's fluttering wave of farewell. In the rear-view mirror she saw Sam make a sceptical little salute.

It goaded her. The next day, in her lunch break, Charlotte went to the boutique with the potted kumquat trees and no price tags and paid the earth for a strapless black dress.

When she saw it, Gale was agog, covetous.

'I bought it on impulse,' Charlotte said, embarrassed now by it.

The admission amazed Gale more than the dress itself. 'Wow! You've changed your tune. Just what went on in the dark between you and sexy Sam?'

'Shivering,' she said dourly, fingering the boning that seemed insecure support for the strapless bodice. She wasn't the type to do without straps or safety ropes. Not in normal circumstances. 'I'll probably never find the nerve to wear it.'

Sam was on television during the week, announcing his retirement from cricket. She was surprised, then admiring. Sam would go down in cricket history as an outstanding player. How difficult it must have been to abandon the dream of being one of the truly great, to turn from the urgings of fans like the Marshall brothers. If he hadn't gone out in a blaze of glory, at least Sam had gone with grace. In the fickle about-face that typified the Australian media, Sam was suddenly a hero again. His loss as the finest fast bowler since Lillee was lamented. He was affectionately recalled as one of the country's outstanding sportsmen, film tributes displayed his unorthodox, athletic technique in slow motion. Sheer poetry in motion, one sports journalist said. Play it one more time, Sam.

A television channel contracted him as a sports presenter. Reputation mended, his son restored to him. Probably Champions stock had gone up as well, Charlotte thought. Sam the builder. The cellar episode really had been the kiss of life to him. Asked in a TV interview about the possibility of a fight with conservationists over Cranston, Sam repeated what he'd told Charlotte. He wouldn't make any decision until experts had gone over the building. 'Unless it collapses in the meantime,' he joked.

'Has Miss Wells pushed you into this?'

Sam looked annoyed. 'Not at all. Ironically, I had already decided to give the old place a second chance while I was trapped in the cellar.'

Of course, he had to say that to save face. Sam, Charlotte decided, wouldn't care to look as if he'd been pressured into anything. Charlotte wondered why she felt so uneasy. The feeling was fanned into suspicion a fortnight later, when Stevie phoned her.

'Did you make this call on your own, Stevie?' she asked, wondering if at any moment Sam's voice might cut in on the line.

'Yes. I told you I can use the phone by myself,' he bragged. 'I can read numbers and your number is in our book.'

'Oh, really?' Did Sam keep all his former lady-friends listed in his book? She didn't ask how Stevie knew which number was hers. Stevie Buchanan was shaping up as something of a prodigy, and a complication. It wasn't in her nature to freeze off friendly four-year-olds, yet she didn't want this to become a habit. Maybe, she thought humorously, she would have to change her phone number. Stevie talked almost non-stop. 'Mummy's in Melbourne and Daddy's going to take me to Taronga Park Zoo tomorrow and he said I could have a ride on a huge tractor one time.'

'Do they have huge tractors at the zoo?' she asked, smiling.

'Not at the zoo. The tractor will be at *our* place. We saw a man on a farm and he's going to give the tractor to Daddy and Daddy will give him some money——' he said, struggling with the concept.

'Hire it, do you mean?' She sat up straight. 'Daddy's hiring a tractor? Why, Stevie?'

'So I can ride it, of course,' Stevie said, mystified at the slowness of adults.

Charlotte's mind raced. What could Sam possibly want with a piece of heavy farm equipment? Only one answer presented itself. The ethics of grilling a four-year-old were dubious, but Charlotte stifled her conscience. 'At your place in the country, Stevie?'

'Yes, where there's a creek with tadpoles. Tadpoles turn into frogs,' he told her confidentially.

'And when did Daddy say he'd take you for a ride on the tractor, Stevie?'

'On Saturday.' His voice dropped to a furtive whisper. 'Mrs Hume's coming. She'll be mad at me for touching the phone——' Some clattering ensued, then the line went dead.

Charlotte chewed her lip. She considered alerting Mrs Fulbright and the Society, but all she had to go on was a hunch and the chatter of a child. She could confront Sam outright. Several times later she picked up the phone and put it down again.

'I'm a reasonable man.' 'Let's hope the old place doesn't fall down in the meantime.' 'Some old heaps don't need any help from bulldozers.' But some did. Sam had certainly planted the seed in people's minds. No one would be surprised if Cranston's remaining structure collapsed. No one would know if someone helped its demise along and who would care, anyway? There was no cause so lost as that of a demolished building. In her mind's eye she saw the old place on its rise, a tractor pushing at its walls, Sam at the controls. Sam the wrecker. The vision caused her physical pain.

'He wouldn't!' she said out loud. But Sam had a ruthless streak and he didn't like people telling him what to do. Charlotte wasn't sure what, if anything, she should do with this inside information. But on Friday night she decided to take a drive in the country. This time she left a note for Gale, taped to her dressing-table mirror.

The early morning mist hung in shreds. When she arrived, it had been thick further along where the road bridged the creek. But now the sun slanted shadows of fenceposts on to the shaggy roadside, revealed the rust on Cranston's old iron gates, dried the dew. Charlotte checked her watch. Seven o'clock. She had been here over an hour. Already she'd walked along the track to

Cranston to check that she wasn't keeping watch over a house already reduced to rubble. But it was still standing, its outer walls untouched by the roof collapse. She took some photographs with the new camera that had been delivered a few days previously with a terse note. 'Check the roof first in future. S.B.' Typical Sam. No apology for the bad temper that had ruined her camera. The man just didn't have a way with words.

She walked down to the creek, approaching the jungle along the banks carefully, lest Sam had set up camp again. But there was no red tent, no bike, no underpants draped on bushes. The peach trees had finished flowering. If there was any fruit on the trees, she couldn't see it. This time she got her photograph of Robert and Emma's inscription and lingered for a while in the place where lovers met. It was with reluctance that she went back to her car.

Another hour passed, and another. Charlotte, tired from her early start, stretched out and dozed on the back seat of her car, parked under the cover of the willow tree. At ten she drank tea from her vacuum flask, then walked down to the bridge. Of course, Stevie might have got it wrong; his tractor ride might be *next* Saturday, or even the one after that. Crouching under the bridge, she watched some minute fish dart about in the water. Now that she was here, it seemed unlikely that Sam would come, sneakily armed for destruction and she felt both pleased and faintly ridiculous.

He came at noon and she almost didn't hear him. She was below the bridge, propped against a tree and drowsing in dappled sunlight. The sound of the motor came gradually, a low throb underscoring the gurgle of water and the high, clear notes of bellbirds. Charlotte scrambled up and saw a massive wheeled machine turn in at Cranston's gates. A man jumped down from the high seat and went to unlock the gates. Even from this distance she recognised Sam's athletic movements. Her stomach knotted. He was actually going to do it.

'Sam!' she yelled. But the motor was running and he
didn't hear. She hauled up the steep bank. Sam swung
the gates open wide. His mouth moved as if he was
whistling or talking to himself. Jauntily he went back to
the tractor, jumped aboard and drove through. By the
time Charlotte ran back along the road, he had relocked
the gates behind him and gone. She rattled the iron gate
bars and watched the tractor move at a cracking pace
along the track, raising dust. 'Sam!' she yelled. But of
course, he didn't hear.

As dust obscured him, she dithered. She had never
planned what she might do if Sam actually came because she'd had some daft idea that, as long as she was
here keeping watch, nothing would happen. That jaunty
walk of his jarred on her. The picture of a man plea-
surably anticipating what he was about to do. Scowling,
she clambered over the fence and set off in the trail of
dust. The motor noise faded and strengthened as the
tractor followed the curving track. Logic told her that
when he reached the house Sam would stop and walk
around a bit to choose his spot. After all, he wouldn't
want to risk being buried in falling masonry again. But
the vision of Sam at the controls, ramming into
Cranston, was too strong for logic. Charlotte put on
speed, leapt off the main track where it turned in a wide
loop and bounded over rough ground to get there first.

Panting, she stumbled up a rise and careered downhill,
faster and faster. Screened at first by a stand of wattle,
the tractor appeared directly in her path and she couldn't
stop. Through the dust she saw Sam's horrified face.
The engine faltered, whined and the machine veered to
one side. Charlotte, hurtling from the slope, passed
within a foot of the massive wheels. Deafened by the
roar, she somersaulted on to the grass on the other side
of the track.

The tractor engine cut out. Dust swirled. Sam sat
frozen on the high seat. He pressed a hand to his closed
eyes and gave his head a shake as if trying to rid himself

of an illusion. When he opened his eyes again she had raised herself on one elbow. White-faced, he stared at her.

'What in God's name do you think you're doing?' he said at last.

Winded, speechless, Charlotte scrambled up and made wild gestures towards the house, pointed at the tractor, shook her head. 'Can't let you——' she croaked and planted herself in front of the machine, arms outstretched in the classic stance of the protestor.

He sat there for maybe twenty seconds grimly following this eloquent piece of semaphore. Charlotte stood her ground in that shrapnel glare.

'Get out of my way, Charlie.' The tone was low, dangerous. But Sam wouldn't hurt her. She looked up at him and wasn't so sure.

'No, Sam. Wait for a while, please, before you do anything. It's so sneaky and underhand and—and unworthy of you and you'll hate yourself for it later, I know you will.'

'I don't need you to save my soul,' he said between clenched teeth. 'Get out of my way.'

'No.'

His jaw clenched. After a few moments he got down. He wore track pants and old sandshoes and a sleeveless T-shirt. Perspiration glistened on his arms. He looked strong enough to knock Cranston down without a tractor. Hands on hips, he studied her with the glowering calculation that had unnerved his opponents on the sports field. And they had at least had protective clothing and a bat to hit with.

'How did you know I'd be here today?' he said.

'Stevie told me about the——'

'Stevie?' His head snapped back. His blue eyes were glacial.

'He phoned me——' she said, meeting his glare of disbelief with a weak, 'He *did*!'

'Do you mean to tell me,' he said, measuring the words out on a slowly rising scale, 'that you've been *interrogating* my son? My *son!*' His shout sent two magpies flapping from the wattle trees. 'Turned a four-year-old kid into a spy against his *father?*'

'Don't be silly, Sam,' she said nervously, backing off a step. 'It wasn't like that——'

'There is *nothing* so dangerous as a do-gooder,' he snarled. 'Next you'll be tapping my phone, all for my own good, of course. All in a good cause. To save my soul.' Without taking his eyes off her he reached into the cockpit and lifted out a coil of rope.

Charlotte took another step back. 'What—what's that for?'

Sam bared his teeth. 'It's for your own good.'

She backed away then turned and ran but she had already run a race and Sam was known for his speed over the ground. He overtook her within seconds, grasped her arm and strode on at a pace that forced her into a canter. Before she caught her breath, Sam hauled her around and backed her against a fig tree. He held her there with his knees while he slipped the rope around her waist.

'Take my advice, angel, and find a guy who can live with your lectures; marry him fast and have some kids. Otherwise you might turn into a meddling, righteous, interfering old biddy.'

Charlotte followed his movement with the rope in astonishment. 'You can't mean to—you *wouldn't* tie me up—it's positively *primitive*—I'll have you charged with assault! How would you like to explain this to the police?'

'"The thing is, Officer,"' Sam said earnestly, '"this crazy woman came running straight at the tractor. There was no guarantee she wouldn't keep on doing it. So I had to—restrain her, for her own good, of course."'

He passed the rope around the tree, binding her to it.

'Sam, you bastard!' she shrieked, reaching around behind the tree trunk for the knot. 'You won't get away with this.'

'"What's that you say, Officer? Do I want to charge the poor, demented woman with trespass?"'

'Damn you, Sam! I don't want to see this, but I'm going to force myself to watch you destroy your heritage so that you might at least feel some shame. How can you have any self-respect, *sneaking* around like this? What will you tell Stevie when he asks what happened to the house—the famous house his forebears built?'

He tweaked the rope. 'It should take you about five minutes to get that knot undone, angel. Meanwhile, you can watch me do what I came to do.'

He gave a patronising little pat to her shoulder and walked away with that same jaunty step.

'Do your worst, Sam! Those walls are a foot thick. You might think you're the Lord High Executioner, driving that piece of machinery, but it'll take more than some tinpot little tractor to move a building that's stood for over a century!'

She screamed the words over the racket of the engine and the truth of them hit her even before she saw that Sam was headed not for Cranston itself, but beyond it. Of course. Those stone walls wouldn't fall to anything but an earthquake or a wrecking ball. Why hadn't she realised that? Because, she realised, it hadn't been Cranston she was worrying about so much as Sam in the role of wrecker. Whether he'd harmed the house or not, the intention to do it would have harmed Sam. And she couldn't stand by and do nothing while Sam came to grief.

In the tractor, Sam circled a dead tree, set the bar against the trunk. The tree trembled and yielded slowly. With a crack it fell. He stopped the machine and got down with a chainsaw. Sam was knocking down trees, not Cranston. Her relief was fleeting. Charlotte closed her eyes, her face suffused. He had come to knock down dead trees and she was capering around like the poor, demented woman he'd mentioned, trying to stop him demolishing a house with a machine that wouldn't even put a dent in it.

She shook off the last shreds of irrationality with the rope. Tossing the cord aside, she looked over at him, still bent over the wood, the chainsaw snarling spasmodically as he cut branches into short lengths. Somehow she would have to squeeze out an apology, she supposed.

He glanced around, saw her approaching and turned off the saw, moved in a leisurely fashion to stow it on the tractor. Doggedly, she ploughed through long grass. If only she'd stayed at home. She could have done her washing and ironing by now. Something sensible.

A few metres away she stopped. Sam looked indolent after all his activity, his body on a slant, propped against the tractor's giant wheel. He was shiny with sweat, dust-smeared and could have used a shave. He should put himself on the Champions Calendar and bring joy to all those mothers who bought junior football boots and tennis racquets. Charlotte fought his advertising appeal.

Sam patted his face with a towel which he slung around his neck. Then he drank from a frosted soft drink can. The soft glugging sound as he swallowed made Charlotte aware of her parched throat. He wiped his mouth with the back of his hand and looked her over, paying special attention to her shirt front.

'Lord High Executioner?' he said, raising his brows.

'Oh.' She was at a loss. Surely someone else must have shouted that emotive term. What was happening to her, to make a raving nitwit of her? Charlotte questioned the tense. Was happening? Had happened?

Sam picked up a hefty length of branch and hit it on the ground. It gave a brittle snap. 'White ants,' he said, conversationally. 'Mrs Hume is bringing Stevie out here this afternoon and I didn't want him to risk an accident. He fancies himself as an expert tree-climber.'

Charlotte took a deep breath. 'You might have explained that you were only going to knock down dead trees.'

'My land. My house. My trees. I don't have to explain.'

'You could have told me when I stopped you on the track.'

'You could have trusted me when I said I would wait for the experts' opinion.'

'Trusted you? You lied to me once; why not again?'

Sam stiffened. A faint flush appeared high on his cheekbones but it could have been because of the sun and exertion.

'I told you no lies,' he said, apparently in no doubt as to what she referred.

'A lie of omission. That's the same. You had the chance to tell me you weren't divorced and you deliberately let me think you were. I'd never trust you again.'

He smiled crookedly. 'I'm getting bruises from falling off so many pedestals.'

'I never put you on a pedestal. You were no hero of mine then and you certainly aren't now,' she said sharply, but she was aware of doubt. Had she fallen into the trap that his fans so often did? Made a hero of him in that cellar—endowed him with all the qualities she valued most in a man, then been furious when he'd turned out to be human? 'Give me one good reason for not telling the truth.'

'You'd just asked me to take you to bed. It didn't seem the time to go into just how dead my marriage was. Finished is finished.' He tossed the now empty drink can in the air and caught it with an overarm swipe. So studiedly offhand, the rat.

'You should have told me. I don't mess with married men.'

'Come on, angel. There were sparks flying between us and there was a chance we could have died down there. Are you trying to tell me that my being married would have made any difference?'

'I *am* telling you.'

'You would have died a virgin?' he mocked.

'And you would have died a married man.' She looked him in the eye. 'Obviously you believed it would have made a difference—or you wouldn't have lied.'

'I wanted you,' he said lightly, tossing the drink can to the side and twisting his other arm behind him to make a fancy catch. 'And you said it yourself, we had a nice mood going, so why risk spoiling it with a lot of technicalities?'

She felt a wild physical response to the first part of his answer, but doused it. Being wanted was merely chemistry. She dealt as summarily with her feeling of disappointment. What had she expected him to say? That he loved her, needed her?

'You look hot. If you want a cold drink, help yourself.' He hitched a thumb over his shoulder at the tractor. 'In the icebox.'

Her thirst was greater than her pride and she clambered up into the cabin of the tractor and took a cold can of lemonade from the Esky. The liquid went down sweetly, dribbled on to her chin in her haste to quench her thirst. 'Ah,' she sighed, tipping her head back and holding the icy can against her cheek. She looked down to find Sam watching her through squinted eyes. Suddenly the heat of the day pressed closer. A crow called and an answer came from a long way off. From the creek came the brief rasping of a frog. 'I must go,' she said inanely, like a guest taking her leave from an afternoon tea.

Sam moved in to help her descend from the tractor. His hands went to her waist but he made no immediate move to lift her down, just stood there, flexing his fingers, looking up at her. There was a smoky, hazy look in his eyes that matched the smudged, blue horizon. She felt the heat coming off his skin, smelled his earthy, male scent that blended with the smell of grass and earth. Sam should always wear a sign, she thought—'roof might

fall'. She made a mental vow to leave Cranston's future
in the hands of Mrs Fulbright and Mrs Humphries and
keep away from Sam.

'How was the movie with good old Brian?' he asked.

'Great,' she said robustly, then spoiled it by adding,
'It was an Italian movie.'

'Ah. That's really living. An *Italian* movie. *La dolce
vita*, angel.'

'Your Italian accent is atrocious. Let me down, please.'

Sam gazed straight ahead at her shirtfront. 'You've
lost a button.'

'Button?' She looked down and saw at last what Sam
had been gawking at. Her shirt gaped open, displaying
her white cotton bra and half her breasts. *'Voyeur!'* she
spat, flushing as she dragged the edges of the shirt
together.

'Your French accent is atrocious.' His eyes were still
riveted to her chest. 'Grrrr. White cotton. What *is* it
about white cotton that's so——?' Sam took a deep
breath and tilted her forward suddenly to land a kiss on
the exposed skin of her chest.

'Don't!' She dropped her shirt to ward him off and
so made two mistakes. Her hands fell on Sam's shoulders
and her shirt flapped free in the breeze, so allowing Sam
to kiss her again. The charge of it ran like a current
through her body.

'Sam,' she croaked.

'Charlie.' He swept the shirt aside and scattered kisses
over her breasts, touching his tongue here and there so
that the breeze cooled each tiny dot of moisture, mapping
out his course. If she joined the dots, would they spell
something? Danger. Roof might fall. She didn't care for
one wild moment with Sam's strong hands on her body
and Sam's mouth on her bare skin and the sun heating
her through and her fingers pushing through his thick,
untidy hair. She sighed and the sound was a breathless,
alien note in the drugged silence.

It sobered her. 'Let me down, Sam.'

He tilted back his head and looked her over. 'Your own mother wouldn't recognise you,' he said, patently pleased with the flushed, rumpled state he had induced. Sheer ego, she thought wrathfully, pushing him aside to jump down. His gaze became thoughtful as he watched her twitch at her gaping shirt and tidy her hair.

'You must have been a real rebel as a teenager—worried your parents sick, I dare say.'

'Why do you dare say that?'

'Most kids want to be different from their folks—want to wear outrageous clothes and shock Mom and Pop with their hair and their taste in music. Poor Charlie,' he said with a laugh. 'Your parents had already grabbed all the anti-establishment attitudes. They were writing the pop music that your peers were rocking to, were wearing the trendy gear and the way-out hair, so I guess you couldn't.'

'No self-respecting teenager wants to look like her mother and father,' she said lightly. The struggle for individuality had been anything but light-hearted.

'I suppose you could have gone one step further to punk gear, or retro,' he said.

'It was the safety pins through the nose that discouraged me.'

'So you went the other way. Conservative, establishment, prim. Must have worried your folks sick, having a prim daughter. Just as worrying as a mini-skirted little rager would be to conservative parents. I'll bet you didn't even like their music.'

She shrugged. 'When you hear it in every stage from composition through to performance, it tends to pall a bit.'

'Let me guess—you used to go to your bedroom and play the classics.'

She turned away to fix her shirt edges together with a safety pin, surprised that he had bothered to give it so much thought. 'That's right,' she said, equably.

'You rebel, you. And no mad hairstyles, I suppose? You never dyed your hair red or bleached it or had a punk cut or blue streaks?'

'Somehow the red, white and blue never suited me.'

'In fact, your parents were more like the kids and you were more like a parent.'

'Well, *someone* had to remember to pay the electricity bill,' she said, 'And buy the groceries and water the garden. Musicians tend to forget little things like that when they're writing new songs or putting down tracks for a new album.' And little things like a daughter, she thought, surprised that it still had the power to rankle. Stars were so self-absorbed. Her mother had phoned to say that Sid, the producer gone walkabout, had been found busking in a country town, as if Charlotte might not sleep at night without the good news that work had recommenced on the album.

Sam studied her thoughtfully. 'It must have been a strange upbringing. Were you a celebrity at school?'

She shrugged again and the thought occurred to her that she was borrowing the movement from Christopher Dunlop. 'I was Earthbound's daughter. Naturally, I got to meet other musicians, and everyone wanted to know about them. My parents used to give me heaps of autographed pictures to give away to kids at school. Once they even came and gave a mini-concert in the school hall to raise money for a new gym.' She smiled. 'Their equivalent of a home-made cake for the cake stall.'

'They had all the adventures, took all the risks, and you kept the home fires burning. The sensible, prudent daughter.'

'Only until I was twenty. Their manager took over all that kind of thing when I moved out.'

'To share an apartment with your cousin,' he mocked. 'Who has all the adventures while you—I'll bet—keep the home fires burning. What's changed? Does she call you Mama?'

She sent him a dark look. 'Not all the adventures. I was the one who was buried alive in a cellar, more's the pity.'

'Not such a pity. You came out more alive than you'd ever been, admit it.'

Charlotte snorted. 'You rate yourself too highly, Sam.'

'But now you're reverting back as fast as you can. That's why you're playing safe with good old Brian.'

Colour sky-high, she turned away sharply and started walking, not choosing a direction, just anywhere out of Sam's vicinity. 'All this psychological analysis is fascinating. I suggest you apply it to your own life. That could stand some scrutiny.'

Her barb didn't strike home. Sam paced alongside her, displaying the single-mindedness that had made him a champion. 'Scared of what might happen if you let yourself go, Charlie?'

Long grass swished around her legs. Back to ordinary life, she'd thought about Brian. She wouldn't have believed Sam perceptive enough to see through it.

'You've rushed right back to the way things were, even rushed back to good old Brian. Because it's safe. He's safe.'

'You're talking nonsense.'

Sam's voice changed down. 'You know you won't wake up a wanton with him, angel. You won't leave scratches on his back and gasp your pleasure out loud and ride like the devil and call out——'

'Stop it!' She halted, glared at him, her fists clenched.

'No,' Sam said reminiscently. 'That wasn't what you said.'

'You are an unmitigated swine——'

'You shocked yourself, didn't you, Charlie?' he said on a gentler note. 'You didn't know about yourself and now you want to back away from it—rationalise it all away. "I thought I was going to die".'

'I did think I was going to die,' she said stiffly.

'But instead you suffered a fate worse than death,' he quipped. Charlotte had a violent need to wipe the smirk from his handsome face. 'You found another side of yourself and now you want to bury it alive again. Not having much success at it, are you?'

Charlotte struck out again into the long grass. 'I don't know what you're talking about.'

'Today. Screaming like a valkyrie. All that heat and passion. Practically throwing yourself beneath the tractor wheels——'

'I was concerned about Cranston, that's all.'

'—running your fingers through my hair, groaning——'

'Oh, shut *up*!'

She stopped, found herself back under the tree where the discarded rope lay in a heap. The track that would lead out to the road was further away than ever. Just once, she thought in frustration, it would be nice if she could pick the right direction.

'I wouldn't like to see you deny that other part of yourself.'

Sam sounded serious, even concerned.

'Careful, Sam,' she chided. 'You're sounding like a do-gooder. What is it to you what I do?'

'There are enough tight-lipped, unfulfilled women in the world. Besides, in a way I feel—responsible.'

Responsible for her blooming into a real woman! Charlotte made some choked, contemptuous noises and said a few damning words about the size of his ego.

'The size of my what?' he asked blandly.

Any other man would have wilted under Charlotte's glare. Sam leaned on the tree and took a penknife from his pocket. Idly, he scratched some lines on the fig's trunk. 'All that heat and passion, Charlie. If I hadn't stopped just now, we'd be making love in the grass.'

The breeze brought goose-bumps up on her skin. Involuntarily, her gaze flicked to the long grass and for a moment she almost caught the image of herself and Sam, making love in the sunlight. 'I wasn't thinking. I was shocked,' she excused herself. 'After all, I'd almost been flattened by a tractor then tied up by a great, hulking, sweaty barbarian and I——'

'"Didn't know what I was doing",' he mimicked. '"Thought I might die". Rationalising again. If I were truly a do-gooder, I'd save you. I'd take you to live with me and make love to you, every night. Well,' he added modestly, glancing around from his scratching on the tree, 'almost every night.'

'For my own good?' Charlotte enquired, but her heart thumped and a new series of images crowded in on her, with tangled bedsheets instead of long grass.

'And mine,' he admitted.

The arrogant swine. *Take* her to live with him. As if he only had to say the word and she would slavishly follow.

'What happened to keeping the *episode* uncomplicated? The big goodbye; it's been fun but let's not spoil it by clinging?'

His eyes narrowed. 'It seemed a good idea at the time. When I saw you again, I wasn't so sure. And today seems to prove that we—haven't come to the end of our interest in each other.' When she didn't speak he smiled complacently and added, 'And you seemed to hit it off with Stevie.'

Charlotte's head snapped up. 'Oh? Is that what qualifies me, Sam? I hit it off with your son?'

'It's one important factor. Stevie will be spending some time with me in future and it's important that he likes anyone—in my life.'

Temper sparkled in her eyes. 'So. I've been cleared by Buchanan senior *and* junior,' she marvelled. 'And I'm allowed to play on the team! Should I feel honoured?'

Sam put away his penknife and flicked irritably at a fly. 'You have a way of twisting things, angel. Stevie's had a rough time this past year. I don't intend to upset him any further by introducing anyone into his life that he doesn't like. When it comes to a choice between any woman and my son, Stevie will win hands down every time.'

'So he should!' It was that 'any woman' that stung her, not his natural protectiveness to his son. She didn't want to be 'any woman', approved because she fitted in. 'You said you wouldn't get involved again,' she said sharply, visited by a sudden, blinding insight into what she did want.

He took another swipe at the fly. 'I don't intend to get involved,' he said, holding her gaze. 'Not permanently.'

'At least you're being honest. On *this* occasion.'

There was a tight look to Sam's jaw. 'What's your answer, angel?'

'You mean this isn't hypothetical? What was the question exactly—move in with me? Let's have an affair, a fling, another *episode*—until we come to the end of our interest in each other?'

He cast his eyes up in exasperation. 'How would you like me to phrase it?'

In words Sam didn't have in his vocabulary. Words like 'need' and 'love' and 'like' and 'share'. 'It doesn't matter. The answer's no.'

He took it like a man. Straightened, stretched. Shoulders bunched, arm muscles rippled and a bone cracked as he flexed his spine. Charlotte averted her eyes from all this male bounty she'd refused. A good thing she had principles.

'Probably just as well. I was already regretting it,' he had the nerve to say. The man wasn't even involved enough to be disappointed at her rejection. Charlotte's pride was in tatters.

'It was academic anyway. I'm not the type to conduct some tawdry little hole-and-corner affair with a married man.'

'Separated,' he corrected her.

'And when I do take a lover it won't be someone like you,' she went on, striving to score a point.

Sam's philosophical air vanished. His eyes narrowed.

'Someone like me? You found me more than acceptable—and more than once, angel.'

Her face flamed. Reckless of her, trying to score points with an experienced player like Sam. He'd had a reputation for sorting out the weaknesses of his opponents and playing tirelessly on them. Endurance, she had discovered from all those television tributes, was something Sam was noted for.

'Time was running out, and you *were* the only man there——' She left the statement stranded on a delicate note.

'No, no—don't try that, angel. It wasn't pure experimentation. You're the kind of girl who has to feel she's in love first.'

'Well, I *did* feel I was in love. At the time.'

'You trusted me to be your first lover.'

'And you were very nice,' she said with an air of being scrupulously fair. 'Very thoughtful and patient and—very nice,' she finished lamely as a blast of Antarctic air came her way.

'Do I get a mark out of ten?' he jeered.

The hapless fly buzzed once more around his head. Squinting fiercely in the sun, Sam tracked it. His hand whipped up in a blur and closed in mid-air. He tossed the stunned fly aside. Then he picked up the rope and strode away, coiling it over his shoulder.

On the tree he had scratched the words, 'Charlie was here.'

'Juvenile,' she said under her breath, and set course for the track. Before she reached it she looked again at Cranston's ruined splendour. Her eyes flicked back to the tractor. The machine would make no impact on the stone walls, but what if he hooked up ropes to some of those remaining interior beams? Sam tossed the coiled rope into the cabin and stood watching her, hands on hips. There was a nasty, comprehending gleam in his eye. 'I feel another lecture coming on. It's a good thing we're alone. I only ever discovered one way to stop you from talking.'

Even for Cranston she couldn't come up with a reply to that. Red-faced, she hastened along the track. She took some wistful pleasure in the fact that, even with beautiful, willing women to choose from again, Sam still wanted her. But not in any serious way. It would make no waves in his life because she'd turned down his proposition. Cranston was silent, empty, the row of arched doorways blazing with light from within where the breached roof let in the sun. Charlotte went past the house quickly. Whatever happened to it, she probably wouldn't see it again. Or Sam, for that matter. But maybe he wouldn't forget about her entirely. *Charlie was here*. Fig trees lived a long, long time and Sam's schoolboyish message would live with it.

The countryside rolled and stretched in hazy earth tones to smudged-in hills on the horizon. How far away were those hills? she thought irrelevantly. How long would it take to come to the end of her interest in Sam?

CHAPTER EIGHT

TEA with Mrs Fulbright and Mrs Humphries was like a trip into the past. Their tea-tray was worn mahogany lined with fresh linen, their lace cloth and bone china all cherished family possessions in their third generation of use. Mrs Fulbright and Mrs Humphries, who had been friends since girlhood, had pooled their meagre resources and their family treasures when they were widowed. The only thing that they disagreed upon, to Charlotte's knowledge, was cricket. It was not unusual for them to invite Charlotte to afternoon tea on a Sunday, but it was unusual for them to give only one hour's notice.

Mrs Fulbright, dignified but pink-cheeked, presided over the teacups; Mrs Humphries made occasional thrusts with plates of scones and iced cakes. At last the courtesies were observed, everyone supplied with refreshment and there was a short, excited silence.

'Cranston is to be restored!' Mrs Fulbright proclaimed.

The announcement spelled the end of polite conversation. The two old friends cut in on each other, spoke over the other in their excitement.

'The most marvellous coup, Charlotte, and we *know* you must have had something to do with it. He said it was while he was in the cellar that he decided not to wreck the house.'

'A very attractive man, isn't he? Cricketers are so often *thick-set* and short and losing their hair but he is quite out of the ordinary. How *did* you talk him into reconsidering, my dear? But of course—all that time together—partners in disaster—er—fairy cake?'

'Cricketers are fine athletes, Dot,' Mrs Fulbright reprimanded her friend. 'And I don't think we need to

128

press Charlotte as to how she—er—persuaded Mr
Buchanan to a change of heart.' If Charlotte had mis-
guidedly made the supreme sacrifice for Cranston's survival, she almost seemed to be saying, they would prefer
not to know the details.

'For such a famous man, he's very sweet. Unusual for
a Taurus.'

'Sweet?' Charlotte said suspiciously, crushing her
pleasure at this confirmed reprieve for Cranston. What
was Taurus the bull up to?

'He's had reports from two architects who judged the
house sound enough for restoration. He has offered us
the use of the coach-house when it has been re-roofed.'

'And access to the family papers and diaries from his
great-uncle's estate.'

'A most accommodating, *modest* man——'

'The restoration to be based on the original plans and
decoration.'

'And a *handsome* donation to come to us in exchange
for the research work on his family records—to facilitate
the restoration, you see.' The sum was said like an in-
cantation. Which it was, really. Sheer magic for the
Heritage and History Society to receive such a sum.

'To be spent on any projects the Society wishes—absolutely no strings. It would be putting it mildly to say
that our committee would be very disappointed if Mr
Buchanan's offers didn't come to fruition.'

'And why wouldn't they?'

A glance was exchanged between Mrs Fulbright and
Mrs Humphries. 'That—rather depends on you,
Charlotte.'

Charlotte tensed. The last time someone had said 'it
depends on you', she had spent four days captive in a
cellar.

'You see, Mr Buchanan wants *you* to do the research
for him. I got the impression that only you would do.
More tea?' Mrs Fulbright lifted the teapot and looked

pleadingly at her as if a refusal of a second cup of tea might be symbolic of worse to come.

Charlotte bit back a word that might have caused a fatality among the bone china. Researching Sam's papers? Delving into his life—*working* for him? Not if she could help it.

'Did my partner in disaster say when he expected to hear from me?' she asked, waiving the second cup of tea. Both ladies looked anxious. The teapot remained hovering hopefully over her cup.

'He'll be at his office every day next week—or he said you could catch him this afternoon, if you're not tied up.'

Charlotte gritted her teeth at this piece of verbatim reporting. What a rat he was. Mrs Fulbright went on to explain that Sam was coaching some junior players at a sports oval and gave directions.

'Is there any—special reason why you wouldn't feel able to do the research for Mr Buchanan?' Mrs Humphries said, tentatively.

Because I think I might be in love with him and it will only get worse if I'm poring over his family diaries and advising what colours his cornices were originally painted. 'I might be too busy,' she said weakly, feeling guilty that they looked so anxious. Refusing more offers of tea and fairy cakes, she went in a high temper, to find Sam.

She parked the car alongside the sports field. Several youths were throwing balls in the practice nets. Three teenage girls in shorts sat on the grass, their bare legs all slanted in the same direction. Charlotte followed the pointers and saw Sam. He was at the wicket, wielding a bat, calling encouragement to a youthful bowler, who nodded, then ran in and loosed a ball. The crack of the bat echoed across the field and several other youths, along with some very junior boys, loped willingly after the ball. In shinguards, wearing leather gloves and stepping widely into the follow-through, Sam looked swashbuckling, more like a medieval warrior than a contemporary man.

He looked up and saw her. The teenage girls all followed his gaze. Sam tucked his bat under his arm and walked over, wiping perspiration from his brow with the back of his glove. He didn't look surprised to see her.

'Liar,' she spat, when he was close enough.

'Very Shakespearean,' he mocked. 'Denouncement on the greensward. I hate your hair like that.'

'No strings, you said. And now you more or less deliver an ultimatum. If I don't do your work for you, the Society gets no money.'

Sam looked reproachful. 'I didn't say that. Your Mrs Fulbright simply assumed I might lose interest if you turned me down and I——'

'And you let her assume,' she finished. 'Yes, you're very good at that, Sam.'

To her surprise, a faint flush tinged his cheeks. He turned slightly away and used his teeth to pull off one of his gloves. 'It's a reasonable request, Charlie,' he said. 'You care more about the old place than anyone else.'

She eyed him disparagingly. 'How can you look two old ladies in the eye and tell them you decided to preserve Cranston while you were in that cellar when you didn't have one good word to say about it?'

'Ah, but you had good words to say about it. Hundreds of them. I thought a few bad ones made things more interesting. You assumed I was a sport jock, too insensitive to appreciate the finer points of heritage, so naturally you believed every one of them.'

'What? You mean—all those things you said about it being a dump and pulling it down the moment you got out was just to stir me up?' He grinned. 'Oh. You pig, Sam.'

'Serves you right. I'd hardly received the deeds to the old place before your Society was pestering me about what I was going to do with it. Uncle Ralph was going to pull it down and I thought at first it would be a good

idea. But then, I went there to hide out and the old place
started to get to me.'

'You mean while you were camped by the creek?'
Charlotte said.

'As early as that. So you can't take the credit for
changing my mind.' He smiled slyly. 'Disappointed?'

It mortified her that she was. Deep down she would
have liked to think that Sam had changed his mind because of her. But it was sheer ego on her part—wanting
to linger on in his memory for something. Idiotic. Now
she remembered that he'd started to tell her something
about Cranston that night at the hospital. Maybe that
he'd been playing devil's advocate all along and in reality was planning to use the old building. Then she'd
rushed in and made her announcement that had made
it look as if Sam was being forced by the weight of public
opinion to change his mind.

'Oh,' she said, dismayed. 'Why did you let me rave
on about the petition and—saving Cranston——'

Sam snorted. 'Was there some way of stopping you?
You made me look like a soulless lout, angel, and I didn't
appreciate it. I could have told you right then that there
was no need to be militant but a man has his pride.' He
reflected a moment. 'And you could have been crushed
by a tractor because of your do-gooding and my pride.'

Charlotte bit her lip. He made her sound dreadful—
an interfering, campaigning woman. She couldn't defend
herself by saying that she wasn't normally like this, that
it was Sam himself who had fuelled much of the passion
she transferred to Cranston. 'I apologise,' she said stiffly.
'I shouldn't have assumed you were an insensitive sport
jock. It is always dangerous to assume.'

He absorbed that with scarcely a flicker of the eyelids.

'So—what's your answer, Charlie? To research or not
to research?'

'Not. Why don't you do it yourself?'

'Have a heart. It's taken me two weeks to look through
one crate of diaries and faded old recipe books.' He paced

alongside her as she headed back to her car, watched by
the collection of youthful cricketers and fans. The invisible woman, she thought, aware that it was Sam who
commanded their attention, aware too that Sam's attention was divided to include his admirers. It was in
the nature of a star. Faded old recipe books. Recipe
books were a kind of history all their own. She could
never resist old letters and diaries. She resisted them now.

'I don't know enough about the period to know what's
valuable and what is just sentimental keepsake,' he said.
'But I did find the diary of someone called Emma.'

Charlotte turned to him eagerly. 'You think it's our—
I mean *that* Emma? The inscription on the tree?'

'"Journeys end in lovers meeting"? Old Bob's
Emma?' he said irreverently, and shrugged. 'Hard to say.
Might be a clue somewhere in the other eleven crates.'

'Eleven!' Charlotte almost groaned. She was hooked
and he knew it. Twelve crates of history and a hand in
Cranston's revival. Maybe the story of Robert and
Emma. Mrs Fulbright and Mrs Humphries would be de-
lighted. Her resistance wavered. Perhaps this was just
what she needed to get Sam out of her system. Instead
of retreating, she could make a frontal attack on the
problem. It would be more courageous.

The teenage girls had rearranged their legs and rubbed
them with oil so that they gleamed in the late afternoon
sun. The youths stood around waiting for Sam's return,
hands on hips in unconscious mimicry of Sam's habitual
stance, and the small boys, thinking he might be leaving,
raced over to the car and asked for autographs. Good-
naturedly he signed a notebook, some tattered pieces of
paper, a T-shirt and one small, freckled forearm. Being
around Sam was a lot like being around her parents.
And if that didn't cure her, nothing would.

Sam signed his name one last time. Smiling, he turned
back to Charlotte. 'What's your answer, Charlie?'

'There is no room for twelve crates at my flat,' she
said truculently.

'So the answer's yes?'

'You know very well it's the one proposition you've made me that I can't refuse.'

His mouth quirked. 'Good. You'll need this.' He pulled a bunch of keys from his pocket, removed two and pressed them into her palm. 'The keys to my place. That's where the crates are stored.'

'Your place?' She was less certain about the merits of a frontal attack. She had pictured herself working in some warehouse space perhaps, or a back room at one of his Champions stores.

'I've had a room cleared out for the crates and a desk put in. You can come whenever it suits you.' He closed her hand around the keys. 'I had intended to give you a key for different reasons but hell, I'm adaptable. I must take after old Tom, Dick and Harry after all.'

Charlotte looked puzzled.

'When the grapes wouldn't grow, didn't they plant apples?'

And what did that mean? He'd lost interest in her as a woman but valued her enthusiasm for Cranston. Good old Charlotte, such a useful, hard-working, enthusiastic girl to have around when you needed a job done. If she was not to be his lover, then she would be his historian. It was good news, of course, that Sam had abandoned any ideas of persuading her to continue their episode. Consider, she told herself, how difficult it would be to de-toxify herself of Sam if he was in a persuasive frame of mind. She dwelt on the benefits of Sam as a business associate and found it unsatisfying. She had a quick vision of opening the door to his house and finding Sam with some exotic woman in his arms.

'I'll work on your blasted documents but I don't want to keep running into you, Sam.'

She regretted the words instantly, as too revealing. But her bluntness appeared only to annoy him. 'Come when the house is empty. I'll be away on business a good deal. I'll let you know in advance.'

'Nor do I want you phoning me all the time,' she said severely.

Sam's eyes narrowed. 'What would you suggest, angel? Carrier pigeon? Would a note be too intimate?'

She wagged the key at him. Sunlight flashed off it. 'And how many of these are there distributed around the place? If I agree to work at your place, are there likely to be—*people* letting themselves in while I'm working? Perhaps you could give me a list, so that I know the legitimate visitors from burglars.'

'If you mean women, you're way off beam. Apart from Mrs Hume, there's only one other woman I trust with a key to my home,' he said, 'And that's my mother.'

Oh, terrific. He was bracketing her with his mother now. Charlotte almost laughed but Sam watched her moodily and there was something vulnerable about him. A sort of defensiveness that made her remember that he was a very private man and cynical about women. Yet now he gave her his key and trusted her with his privacy. It made her special, she supposed, but she refused to be carried away with delight. Sam's trust was another link in the chain that bound her to him and she'd be better off without it.

Charlotte took her own key-ring from her pocket and slipped his house keys on it. 'Very well,' she said briskly, 'I can only give you two hours a week for the next six weeks until the exams are over and school breaks for the Christmas holidays. I'll want to be paid for my time, of course, quite apart from the donation to the Society. And there's the cost of petrol, too.'

He seemed taken aback at this. Arrogant devil. A few historical crumbs he'd tossed her and he was sure she would slave willingly for him. A labour of love, in more ways than one.

'I'll leave a bill on the desk from time to time. I'd prefer to be paid by cheque.'

She got into the car and closed the door emphatically.

'You can water the pot plants too, then, if I'm paying,' he said, eyes squinted in amusement.

'Pot plants are extra.'

His laughter floated in through the window. Charlotte drove away, glancing in the rear-view mirror to see him walk across the green, swinging the bat in practice swipes. Sam had organised everything to suit himself and already forgotten her. And she, who needed to apply herself to achieve that enviable state, was driving away with the keys to his home. 'Courageous!' she muttered in disgust, wondering how she had the gall to stand up in a classroom and teach adolescents.

CHAPTER NINE

SAM tossed down his bags, picked up the collected mail that Mrs Hume had left for him and went through to the large study full of crates and shelves. He told himself he was keen to see what progress Charlotte had made with the records. But his eyes didn't go to the shelves where she had sorted his papers over the past six weeks; they went to her desk. When he saw the folded note propped up against her tub of sharpened pencils, he grinned and quickened his pace.

About to pick up the note, he stopped, irritated by his eagerness. 'Dammit. I'll have a drink first.' It was said in the spirit of defiance that bothered him, too. Turning his back on the note, he went through to the drinks cabinet in the living-room, trickled some Scotch over ice. Sprawled on the couch, he fanned out the fistful of letters, separating the personal from the junk. He tried to get interested in reading them, but his attention wandered to Charlie's letter.

He wrote to her whenever he had to go away, so that she knew when the house would be empty. Brisk notes at first. 'Away two weeks as from Friday 8th. Sam.' Gradually, though, he'd taken to adding things that would mean nothing to anyone but Charlie. Like when he played in an invitation match between retired professionals and politicians. 'Played the Prime Minister's Eleven in Canberra last week,' he wrote once. 'Your minister was there—the one who likes to hand out special holidays to schools. I bowled him for a duck. Serves him right.'

Another time he enclosed a magazine article praising his decision to retire, commenting on his voluntary work with kids and his new, peaceful image. 'Keeping *my* promises,' Sam had scrawled on the margins of this cutting. 'I'm being nice to the Press and doing something positive for the sport,' and, to remind her of her own promises, made in the cellar, 'How's *Haunting Old Houses* coming? Travelled anywhere lately?'

Charlie had replied, 'Two chapters complete, publisher mildly interested. Walking the Milford Track, New Zealand, in January.'

Sam took a mouthful of Scotch, let it slip slowly down. Trust Charlie to home in on the journalist's passing observation. Was she going alone to New Zealand, or was she going with good old Brian? He might be the type for an outdoors holiday—a man who attended natural health seminars. Sam thought of Charlotte, striding along the Milford Track in her army boots, taking photographs and notes. She was the type who took lots of notes and identified birds. Very stuck on details, Charlie was, very picky. Pedantic, even.

He swirled his glass and the ice clinked. It would have been no bed of roses, getting involved with someone as intense as Charlie. He must have been mad even to have suggested it. Imagine coming home to find that one of her snotty-nosed protégés had slashed his tyres, or that she was up in arms about some other old building. He got up and put one of his old Earthbound records on the turntable. Nowadays he listened more carefully to the lyrics for clues to Charlie's past.

A supremely uncomfortable woman to live with even for a short time, Charlie. This was just the way he liked it. Peace and quiet, no emotional strings. Business trips that didn't turn into guilt trips. Thank God she'd turned him down. He frowned and opened a few of the letters. After he'd finished his drink, he transferred his luggage to the bedroom. In his last note to Charlie he'd said, 'Builders erecting scaffolding around Cranston. Original fireplace found behind panelling in drawing-room as you expected. Roof on coach-house in one month. Tell the old biddies at the next meeting. P.S. Are you going to

risk the Milford Track alone, or playing safe with good
old Brian? P.P.S. What will I do in a drawing-room? I
don't like drawing.'

Sam mooched along to the large study that smelled
of musty old paper. He tugged his tie loose, unbuttoned
the neck of his shirt and reached for Charlie's note. The
news about Cranston would have pleased her. Sam
smiled, anticipating her response to it, suddenly keener
than he ought to be to know if she was going to New
Zealand alone. Maybe she'd tell him to mind his own
business. Maybe he didn't really want to know.

Sam frowned down at the piece of paper. It was an
itemised bill. '''For services rendered——''' he read out
loud. She'd even listed an extra amount for watering the
pot-plants. Sam turned the paper over, hoping for a few
words scrawled on the back—at least a comeback on his
corny joke about the drawing-room, but there was
nothing. Almost he could hear Charlie saying in that
tone she fondly thought of as stern, 'Mind your own
business, Sam.' He felt let down, deprived somehow; his
pleasure in coming home went flat. He tossed the bill
back on to the desk. On the way out he kicked the waste-
paper basket.

School wound up for the summer holidays, and elated
senior students, finished with school forever, threw paint-
bombs and wrote rude remarks on each other's T-shirts
and the lavatory walls while exhausted teachers packed
up their belongings with the usual mixed feelings of
achievement and failure. In the week that followed, Gale
went to Noosa for her holidays, the Heritage and History
Society went into summer recess and Charlotte turned
twenty-three. She celebrated with some teaching friends,
including Brian. Her parents sent her a sheaf of exotic
flowers and a magnum of French perfume. The card
read, 'Darling Charlotte, with heaps of love from Linda
and Martin. P.S. We're staying on in Los Angeles and
won't get home in time for Christmas. Back to finish

the new album. We've written a song about your hummingbirds forgetting the words!'

Sam sent her a present too, several days after her birthday. A pair of grey Bunyip walking boots. The note with them said, 'Wear these instead of the army boots. At least when they find you in New Zealand you won't have blisters. Sam.' A sneaky double allusion to her poor sense of direction and her thriftiness. 'They won't fit,' she said to Gale, who had seen the Champions sticker on the boot box and had drawn her own conclusions.

'Well, well—*another* present from sexy Sam.'

'I told you. The camera he owed me because he wrecked mine. The boots——' She shrugged.

Gale had a speculative look in her eye. 'What's going on between you and him? All those visits to his place—now gifts.'

'For heaven's sake! It's not as if it were diamonds or black garter belts,' Charlotte said huffily. 'They're walking boots and they won't fit and I'll send them back.'

Later she tried them. They fit perfectly.

She spent Christmas Day with Gale's parents. Uncle Simon wore a silly hat as usual and Aunt Frances anxiously checked the food lest she run out of sustenance for the assortment of invited relatives.

'It's Mum's way of saying she cares, you know,' Gale said as she refused for the fourth time an offer of her mother's Christmas shortbread. 'Food is the way she comforts us all. I hardly like to say no, but if I didn't I'd weigh a ton.'

There were eighteen people for Christmas dinner. Afterwards they crammed into the living-room to watch a video of Martin and Linda playing acoustic guitars and singing traditional Christmas carols and a soft, sweet song of their own called 'Hummingbirds have forgotten the words'. 'Merry Christmas, Charlotte, darling. See you in the New Year,' they called, smiling, at the end of the tape. 'Merry Christmas, everyone.' Aunt Frances must have seen the tears in Charlotte's eyes, because she hurried over with Christmas cake and comfort.

Christmas passed. Charlotte went to a New Year's Eve party and was kissed by a lot of people she would have preferred not to be kissed by. How easy it was to get things you didn't really want, she thought. None of her resolutions were new. She had more than enough left over from the old year.

Armed with introductions and recommended sights from Mrs Fulbright and Mrs Humphries, she flew to New Zealand. After a week of touring, she spent three days in Fiordland National Park walking the beautiful, rugged Milford Track. Rain and wind made the going rough over Mackinnon Pass, sandflies found any tiny area of skin unpainted with repellant, dry creeks suddenly filled and had to be waded through. But the rewards were great. Beech forests, draped with mosses and ferns, looking like the scene of Arthurian legends. Sutherland Falls, spilling out from a high granite basin down a thousand metres with its rainbow ending. Rainforest, misty mountain peaks and glacial valleys. Sam's boots were supremely comfortable.

Back home in Sydney, she worked on her book for several days then went to Sam's house. His last note, before Christmas, had been fairly curt. 'Away two weeks from 18th January. Taking Stevie to my mother's.' Sam included his mother's Queensland phone number, presumably in case his house was burgled or she had some urgent need to confer with him about his family history.

His house was open-plan, uncluttered areas with large, squashy leather chairs, space-age kitchen and bathrooms and a fabulous wall of glass fronting on to a courtyard. There was a fully equipped gym with shelves of trophies and sporting awards, casually adjoining a living-room with several modern sculptures and heaps of expensive video and sound equipment. She'd noticed that several of Earthbound's albums were among his record collection. Funny to think of Sam, listening to

her parents' music for years, therefore knowing things
about her even before he met her.

Mrs Hume, the housekeeper, came in once a week to
dust and polish while Sam was away. The place always
looked impersonal and perfect, the way a house could
only look when it was empty. It never varied, not by so
much as the placement of a trophy or a pot plant, and
Charlotte had become so accustomed to it that she
noticed the difference immediately.

Keys in hand, she stopped, gazing around at the huge
living space. A cushion, normally plumped up on a
leather couch, was on the floor. A low-hung picture was
crooked and that wasn't all. One of the glass sliding
doors on to the courtyard was ajar. Someone had got
inside the house. The thought no sooner crossed her mind
before she heard sounds. Her hand went to her throat.
Burglars? Should she tiptoe out and phone the police?
But it could be Mrs Hume, working late. Adrenalin
pumping through her system, Charlotte picked up a
much autographed cricket bat from Sam's trophy collection and followed the sounds. They led her to the main
bathroom door. Taking a deep breath to steady herself,
she hoisted the bat over one shoulder, turned the
doorknob slowly to its limit, then flung the door open.
'Is that you, Mrs Hume?'

All the sounds stopped dead except for a faint, delicate
popping sound. An iridescent bubble floated towards
Charlotte. Two pairs of eyes gazed at her from the large,
Roman-style bath that was topped with froth.

'Oh,' she said weakly, reddening. 'Sam.'

Sam looked her over, taking his time. 'You're always
catching me in the act of cleaning off the grime. I wonder
if it's symbolic?'

She opened and shut her mouth, eventually said, 'Oh,'
again.

Sam grinned. 'Surprised to catch me in the bath with
someone?'

The someone was Stevie. He held a bubble pipe in one hand and a plastic model of a power boat in the other.

'Brrrm, brrrm. Hello, Charlie,' the little boy said. 'What are you doing with that bat? Come and see my boat. Come on.' He beckoned her, palm up, like a traffic policeman. Like father, like son.

Her eyes went to the elder Buchanan. Sam was lounging back, arms braced on the side of the circular bath. His shoulders and biceps were outlined beautifully against the pale tilework, his tan skin glistening. A fleck of froth slipped slowly down his chest. Charlotte had to drag her gaze from its progress over the fabulous contours. Sam's eyes were a startling blue, full of enjoyment at her melodramatic entrance.

'Caught me with my rubber duckie again, angel.' He appeared to remember then that, like his son, he too held a toy plastic boat. Rather sheepishly he let it sink into the suds.

'I thought you were at your mother's place,' she said. 'When I saw the courtyard door open and heard odd noises——'

'You came in to bat against intruders. That's a valuable bit of willow you were about to belt someone with,' he pointed out. Hastily she lowered the cricket bat, glanced down to see that among the signatures were some legendary names. 'My mother's stepson came down with mumps, so we couldn't go there after all.'

'Charlie, do you want something aslutely marvellous?' Stevie enquired. 'Hold out your hands if you do.'

She hesitated, wanting nothing more than to make her escape. But Stevie had his hands behind his back and was delightedly waiting to surprise her. 'How could I pass up something absolutely marvellous?' Tucking the bat under her arm, she complied. Stupid of her, she decided, as she crouched down beside the bath, conscious of Sam so close and the illusion of decency a matter of froth and foam.

'Here they come.' Stevie blew a great cloud of bubbles at her. 'Catch them, Charlie. There's a hundred of them. A hundred's a century,' the cricketer's son informed her. The little boy saw nothing odd about a woman watching him and his father in the bath. Maybe he was used to it, she thought sourly. But that wasn't quite fair. Since the rescue there had been no pictures of him with women, no hint even of anyone in his life. It might mean Sam was being discreet, of course. She made a pretence at catching the bubbles and Stevie chuckled as each one burst. His eyes widened when she managed by dint of great delicacy to catch one lone bubble. It swayed gently on the back of her hand. She showed it to Stevie.

'You're clever,' he conceded, then burst it with a flick of his finger. His triumphant laughter echoed around the bathroom. The water surged and the foam parted. Hastily, Charlotte got up to go.

'Not going to turn tail and run because we're home, are you, angel?' Sam said. 'Just carry on as usual.'

Her eyes sparkled. 'I was going to say the same thing. Don't stop playing with your boat just because I'm here.'

Sam made as if to stand up and suds went streaming downwards. She beat a hasty retreat. 'Brrrm, brrrm,' she heard Sam say, much louder than was necessary. He'd found his boat, apparently.

At least one hour of work before she left, she promised herself. Her self-esteem demanded it. It would look too emotional to run away, too involved. Charlotte closed the door so that she couldn't hear the frolicking in the bathroom and took a stack of old journals and set to work identifying the writers on the family tree diagram she had taped to the wall behind her. Emma and Robert were not on it. She still didn't know where they fitted in, if indeed they belonged to the family at all. The Emma who wrote the diary was married to someone called William. Charlotte hoped it wasn't the same Emma. She wanted to believe that Robert and Emma had enjoyed a long life with each other.

When the door opened, she said blandly, 'Yes?'

But then she looked up and blandness was all but impossible. Sam leaned in the doorway with the lack of self-consciousness of a man totally at ease with his own body. He wore a tan towelling robe several sizes too small for him. His superb chest muscles with their fuzz of dark hair were showcased in the V and the hem came no further than halfway down his thighs. His dark hair flopped damply over one brow, his eyes gleamed a piercing blue.

'How's the *human* restoration business going?' he said mockingly. 'Did Christopher Dunlop like *Famous Bridges of the World*?'

'He burned it,' she said shortly.

'What?' Sam stared. 'Burned the book? Why, the rotten little—how do you know he burned it?'

'He did it in the school grounds, close enough for me to see him, far enough away so that I couldn't stop him.'

'Christopher Dunlop—burning his bridges,' Sam said in wry humour. 'The dumb kid. I guess you really did give up on him after that.' She didn't answer and Sam's eyes narrowed. 'No, of course you didn't.'

'It's all academic now. Christopher's gone and he won't be coming back to finish high school. The last I heard, he was on the dole.' She shrugged. 'You win some, you lose some.'

'Ah, hell, Charlie. I'm sorry. I know how much that meant to you.'

Tears stung her eyes and she struggled to maintain the pretence of professional detachment. 'I'm disappointed, of course, but that's part of being a teacher.' Standing abruptly she went to the shelves, groping in her pocket for a tissue to wipe her eyes. Silly to be upset now, when she'd accepted it so philosophically at the time. It was Sam's empathising that had set her off. She couldn't find a tissue.

'Here.' Sam turned her around and guided her head to his towelling-clad shoulder. 'Cry all you like,' he invited. 'The robe's fully absorbent.'

She gave a hiccup of laughter at that but cried again, holding on to Sam as he wrapped his arms around her. 'I went to see Mr Dunlop again,' she sniffed, her cheek laid against Sam's chest. 'He said I was an interfering, smarty-pants do-gooder.'

'Well, he's right,' Sam said. 'Good intentions don't give you the right to butt in.'

'Oh, thanks for that!'

'That's what friends are for.'

'Friend, Sam? Have you ever been friends with a woman? Especially one who——' She flushed.

'Works for me?' he finished, grinning. 'It's a whole new experience. How was New Zealand? Any earthquakes while you were over there?'

'Green. Lush. Beautiful. No earthquakes.'

'Ah. Brian didn't go with you, then,' he said with a smirk.

She disengaged herself with dignity. 'Thank you for the boots. They were excellent.'

Sam acknowledged the sidestep with a curious little inclination of his head. 'Doing anything on Sunday?'

Her heart raced as if she were an adolescent again, being asked for a date. 'Why?'

'Why don't you come out to Cranston—take a look at the builders' progress? I could use some help in figuring out where the old vineyards used to be.'

The crazy pace of her heartbeat slowed. She was useful to Sam, that was all. 'I charge double rates on Sunday,' she said.

Sam glowered. 'I thought you might enjoy it. I thought you might come as a—friend.'

In spite of herself, she liked the sound of it. 'Why do you want to know about the vineyards?'

'Oh—just for the record.' He shrugged, but when she
unearthed one of the original wine bottle labels from her
files he pored over it.

'Is your family history getting to you at last, Sam?'

He looked up and smiled. 'It must be. I'll provide the
food. I owe you a picnic lunch. Pick you up around
eleven?'

Stevie ran in then, naked and still wet from the bath,
the bubble pipe in his hand, a towel dragging behind
him. Sam grabbed him, tossing his sturdy little body up
into the air, then held him upside down. 'Do it again,
Daddy,' Stevie commanded in what was clearly a ritual,
and Sam obliged. Their voices were a perfect blend—
the teasing rumble of the man's, the treble arpeggios of
the child's laughter. Charlotte turned away to tidy up
her desk. She seemed destined to be an audience of one
to perfect duets.

'Charlie's coming with us tomorrow,' Sam told his son.

'Goodie. You can take pictures of me running fast.
Are you sleeping here tonight, Charlie?' he added
ingenuously.

'No, Stevie.'

'Why not?'

Sam's eyes mocked her. 'He's four. Keep it simple.'

She cast him a darkling look. 'I have to go home to—
er—water my pot plants. Goodnight, Stevie.'

They went to the door with her. Charlotte was rather
desperate to get away from the two near-naked
Buchanans, both just as devastating in their way. Stevie
discovered a trace of detergent remaining in the pipe and
blew bubbles at her as she went through the door. This
time she didn't try to catch them.

The day at Cranston was the first of several that summer.
From a distance the old house looked grand except for
the toothpick structure of scaffolding around it. The
weather was hot and dry, the sky unbroken blue. The
landscape drowsed in the glare, cicadas shrilled in the

thickets by the creek. They ate lunch by the creek, which was not much more than a trickle after months of dry weather. Charlotte thought of it, deep and bottle-green as she'd first seen it. Remembered the first moment when Sam had entered the picture. Her gaze strayed to Robert and Emma's inscription on the tree.

'According to one of your old diaries, the creek used to flood frequently. The bridge across the road had to be rebuilt twice,' she said pedantically, to counter the magic of the place. 'Pipes were run down to the creek further along somewhere and a pump was installed to take water up to the vineyard.'

It was the kind of data that would have made his eyes glaze over once, but now Sam showed enthusiasm. They pushed their way through the creek-bank tangle, looking for pipes, but found none to pinpoint the location of the original vineyards. Later, Charlotte took photographs of Cranston, and of Stevie collecting tadpoles in a jar, and Stevie on the undulating slopes, running fast as he'd promised. The little boy climbed trees too. 'What's written on this tree?' he demanded, seeing the scratched message.

'Charlie was here,' Sam said, slanting a quizzical look at Charlotte. She felt all tied up without any ropes.

'Put my name there, too,' his son commanded. 'And yours, Daddy,' and Sam picked up a stone to add 'Stevie and Sam' to the message. Maybe in years to come someone would think it was the names of three boys. Fig trees lived for hundreds of years. She wished her name weren't on this one.

By mid February the new school year was well under way and work began on Cranston's roof. Mrs Fulbright organised a working bee the day the coach-house was ready for occupation and one of the society members picked up a ragged piece of paper. On one side was written, faintly, 'SOS. Alert police. Trapped in cellar, Cranston, Hawker Road. Sam Buchanan, Charlotte

Wells. 13th September——' On the other was Alice
Cooper's black eye. 'Friday the thirteenth,' Charlotte
said lightly, aware that her colleagues were curiously
awaiting her reaction. 'I should have worn a good luck
charm.'

Life was even, pleasant. Charlotte went out once with
a man she'd met on the plane coming back from New
Zealand, had an occasional dinner with Brian. She didn't
see Sam for weeks at a stretch, and when she did he was
edgy and tense, the relaxed drowsiness of summer already
a memory. He was no longer wearing his wedding-ring
by the time she read that his divorce had been finalised.
Sam didn't phone to tell her about the divorce or anything else, and he didn't write. Why should he? What
was a divorce between friends? But, as she sensed a
growing distance between them, Charlotte stopped
leaving notes on the desk.

She threw herself into the challenge of a new set of
students, she started a new, ambitious wall-hanging at
quilting classes, planned next year's holiday in America.
The publisher's mild interest in her book firmed and she
went to work on it in earnest. Her life was full and challenging and she felt lucky. The hollow feeling that crept
up on her sometimes would pass, she reasoned.

CHAPTER TEN

IT WAS April before Charlotte saw Sam again.

It was a windy, drizzly night. She went with Brian to
see a French film, invited him in for coffee afterwards.
As he started on his third cup of coffee and another
serious attempt to analyse the film, Charlotte stifled a
yawn. Brian was a very nice, *good* man but sometimes
boring. Much of the humour of the film had eluded him
and her enjoyment of it was fast fading as he dissected
it.

When the doorbell rang then, at ten minutes past midnight, she leapt to her feet.

'Funny time to call,' Brian said, miffed because he'd
just got started on the director's true intentions with the
film. 'You don't have to answer it.'

But if it delayed the director's true intentions she was
all for it. She opened the door, peered through the gap
bridged by the safety chain. A tall figure in shades of
grey. Her heart gave a lurch. Charlotte switched on the
light and the shades of grey lit up to tan and darkest
brown and a touch of blue the nearest colour to a summer
sky. She never could decide whether Sam was more devastating in colour or monotone. Was he frowning, or
smiling? 'Sam?' she said uncertainly. She had a strong
impression of desolation, but it was gone in a second
and she blamed it on the bleak weather. His grin was
broad, crinkling up his eyes. Hand on hip, his jacket
slung over his shoulder, Sam had a swaggering look
about him. With a sudden flourish he presented her with
an apple.

'Apple for the teacher,' he said.

Her spirits lifted. With Sam she was stifling laughter,
not yawns. 'You're drunk.'

'As a lord.' Sam performed an unsteady, elaborate bow. Another tenant went past, turning around curiously when he recognised Sam.

'You'd better come in,' she said, grabbing his arm. 'Otherwise you'll be plastered on the front page of the newspapers again.'

'Instead of just being plastered,' he quipped. Over her shoulder he saw Brian and his grin faltered a moment, then broadened. He went to the other man, shook his hand with great affability. Charlotte viewed the practised public relations with suspicion.

'I'll make some more coffee,' she said.

'You know the way I like it, angel.' Sam sprawled on the couch in a familiar manner. He kicked off his shoes, laid back and clasped his hands behind his head. Grimacing, he ran his tongue over his teeth. 'I hope I left a toothbrush here—I'm going to need it in the morning.'

Brian stood up stiffly. Sam returned Charlotte's glare with a lazy smile. 'Don't look so worried, angel. Brian's a man of the world. He understands these things.' He looked at Brian. 'You know how it is. There we were in that cellar—two red-blooded people, sharing a narrow bunk, thinking we might never see the light of day again——' He shrugged.

Bright patches of colour showed in Brian's cheeks. 'Am I to understand——?' he began.

'There, I *told* you he'd understand,' Sam cut in, beaming. 'Been to see a film tonight?'

Charlotte clenched her fists, glowered at him. Her voice came out in a squeak. 'You—you——'

'European film? Great. Come here and say hello, angel.' One of those long arms whipped out and scooped her down on to the couch. Sam kissed her on the mouth with great gusto. 'Don't feel you've got to dash off, Brian——' Sam looked up as the door slammed. 'Oh, darn it, he's gone. Was it something I said?'

Arms and legs furiously scrabbling for balance, Charlotte got nowhere. Her dress was up around her thighs, her hair all over her face. 'You lousy, rotten, selfish pig, Sam!' she yelled, 'How dare you come here and interrupt my private life like this?'

Sam threw one leg over hers, frustrating her attempts to get her feet on the floor. 'Private life—with good old Brian?' he laughed, nuzzling in to kiss her ear. 'Come on, Charlie. You're too much woman for him. Mmm, you smell like flowers in the rain.'

She quelled her response to the touch of his mouth and the beguiling dash of poetry. 'Brian suits me just fine!' Charlotte conveniently forgot the galloping boredom of Brian's film analysis. 'And what makes you think I'm not already *involved* with him? Maybe he's left *his* toothbrush here!'

Sam's head came up suddenly. He searched her face with a sort of muzzy intensity, a frown drawing his brows together. Whatever he saw cleared his expression. 'No,' he said, with a complacent smile that made her want to scream.

She planted her hand on his chest and straightened her arm, giving herself a much needed space. 'If you imagine I'm living some cloistered existence, think again, Sam. I don't consider being deflowered by Sam Buchanan as such a sacred occasion that I'll never take another lover!'

His jaw clenched but, aggravatingly, in a second or two Sam smiled. 'Take another lover. Just don't take good old Brian.' He dipped his head again to her neck, planted a smacking kiss there and made a provocative sortie down into the gaping V of her neckline.

'Stop doing that! Let me go, you big oaf!' Charlotte yelled, weakening as he kissed the hollow at the base of her throat. Her hand, flailing around to find leverage, found his hair instead. She took a handful with the intention of tearing it out by the roots if necessary, but it was thick and damp with rain and it slipped through her fingers somehow and she forgot about intentions. Sam gathered her in fiercely and kissed her, tipped her head back with the pressure of it, and coaxed her lips apart. 'Charlie——' he said huskily, turning her aside to press his mouth to the nape of her neck. She felt the soft slide of her dress zip-fastener and roused herself to push him away, but Sam kissed her neck again and she thought, Just this one kiss, then she would stand up. Her hands travelled over his chest and she thought, Just one moment more of Sam's chest and she would leap from the couch. Sam's mouth trailed fire from her shoulders on to her chest. He tugged her dress down and nuzzled between her breasts and she thought, Why not love him just once more? Who cared? Two adults who wanted each other. That was enough reason for most people. Desire provided all the glib arguments and her body was already humming, anticipating Sam's loving before she answered her own questions. She cared. And desire wasn't quite enough reason for her.

'No.' She pushed him away, sat up and fixed her clothes, embarrassed when she realised how abandoned she looked. Sam gave her a broad smile. His eyes were heavy-lidded, warm, amused. The conquering male, she thought sourly, or very nearly.

'I had too much drink and didn't know what I was doing,' Sam said provocatively. 'What's *your* excuse, Charlie?'

'For the sake of our friendship, Sam, I think we should pretend that didn't happen.'

'Yes, Miss Wells,' he mocked. 'Shall I write it out one hundred times, Miss Wells? "I did not kiss Charlie's neck and I did not kiss Charlie's——"'

'Sam!' She scowled. 'Sit down. I'll make some black coffee.' To sober them both up, she thought.

But Sam didn't sit down. He followed her to the kitchen and propped himself in the doorway, watching her fill the kettle and take down cups. His crumpled clothes and five o'clock shadow gave him a rakish look.

The top three buttons of his shirt were undone. For the life of her, Charlotte couldn't remember unfastening them. 'You look like a seedy private eye from an old movie,' she said sharply. Sam polished the apple on his trouser-front, as if it were a cricket ball, then took a large bite from it. As he chewed, he gave a lopsided grin, but that first impression swept back suddenly. 'What's wrong, Sam?'

His smile disappeared. The jaunty pose became suddenly tense. He squared his shoulders and tipped his head to stare her down, disguising his feelings. But the mask slipped away, leaving his eyes full of hurt and misery.

'Ruth got married today.'

Charlotte checked, the sugar bowl in her hand. A cold, jealous rage overtook her. She was tempted to throw the basin and its contents at him. Wouldn't that be bad luck? Spilled sugar everywhere. 'Is that why you've drunk yourself into this state, Sam? Is that why you're here?' She gripped the basin tight with both hands. 'To cry on my shoulder and seek a little distraction because your ex-wife has married again?'

Sam gazed at the floor as if he hadn't heard what she said. 'Jim Merrick—that's the guy she married. He's a stockbroker.'

Charlotte banged the coffee-pot on to a tray. He could have two cups of the stuff, then she would call a cab and get rid of him. There was a limit to friendship, and she was damned if she was going to listen to his drunken, maudlin ramblings about his ex-wife.

'I wonder what Stevie will call Merrick,' Sam said in a hollow voice.

Charlotte's anger collapsed. Here was what really troubled Sam. He raised agonised eyes to her. 'He wouldn't call him "Daddy", would he?'

She bit her lip. 'Is Stevie—staying with them?'

Sam nodded, ran a hand through his hair leaving it standing on end. 'I agreed not to see him for a while— give him time to get used to Merrick. Then he'll come to me for a month. I don't know if we're doing the right thing by the kid, messing him about like this all the time. Maybe I should let him stay with them permanently.'

It was a measure of his love that he could even consider giving up Stevie if it was better for the boy. She was angry with him still, but her heart ached for him.

She took the coffee into the lounge. Sam sank back on the couch and closed his eyes. 'I'm glad you were home, Charlie. I needed you tonight.' His eyes flickered open. 'I needed to talk to you,' he added, diluting the statement.

A mirthless laugh stuck in her throat. Needed. There were certain things she had to have from the man she would spend her life with, she'd always thought. He had to be a friend, he had to respect her, trust her, need her, love her. Four out of five—you've just missed out on a perfect score, Miss Wells, so you don't take home the grand prize. Levelly, she said, 'You can talk freely, Sam. Gale isn't here.'

But he didn't talk. His breathing deepened and Charlotte hesitated about phoning for a cab. Weakly, she let twenty minutes pass, aware that Gale might come home at any moment. She would never hear the end of it if her cousin found Sam sprawled here, tousled and scruffy and magnetic even in sleep. Determinedly, she looked up at the taxi service number, jotted it down with a pencil.

Sam opened his eyes and stared at the ceiling. 'I wonder if it would have been a boy or a girl.'

'What?'

'If we'd had a baby.'

Charlotte almost broke the pencil in half. 'What did you say?'

'I was relieved when you said you weren't pregnant, but now I almost wish you had been.'

She gaped at him.

'I would have liked another child,' he said with a sigh. 'I was thinking about it after I said goodbye to Stevie.'

Charlotte stiffened. Anger started deep down in her, a lick of flame that caught on the dry tinder she'd carried around for years. She walked over and stood in front of him. 'It might interest you to know that I don't share these maudlin fantasies of yours,' she said, snipping the words out in barely controlled savagery. 'It's tough knowing that Ruth has remarried, so you come here thinking of me as—as some kind of substitute. You're missing your son and now you wouldn't mind someone else to call you Daddy. Well, let me tell you, Sam, no child of mine would ever have been used as a substitute for another. No child of *mine* will ever be second-best to anyone or—anything, and neither will I!'

Sam winced at her outburst, held up a hand peaceably. 'Just conjecturing, Charlie——'

'Oh, yes?' She set her hands on her hips. 'And where in your *conjecturing* do I fit in? Would I have borne this love-child to replace Stevie, then conveniently faded off the scene?'

'Don't be a fool, Charlie. I would have married you.'

'*Would* you indeed?' she said dangerously, pacing the floor. 'You're not the remarrying kind, but you would have married me, whom you don't love, in order to be Daddy to a child who would have been an understudy to Stevie? Second-best, all the way down the line! And I'll bet you think I would have jumped at it!'

He remained unperturbed. Hands linked behind his head, he gave her a heavy-lidded smile. 'If I asked you, would you marry me now, angel?'

She stopped dead in her tracks, heart thumping crazily until common sense prevailed. It was quite amusing, really. *If* I asked you. Sam might be drunk and indiscreet, but his wariness was undiminished. Angel. Charlie. Was there some significance in which name he chose to use? Did he choose to call her 'Charlie' when he was being sincere, and 'angel' when he was not? Marry him? She might as well become a private eye, always looking for clues as to whether he was sincere, whether deep down he might love her, and how deep that love went. Oh, no. She'd been there, done that.

'We've got a great thing going here. We can rebuild Cranston together. We're great in bed,' Sam reflected. 'We could have kids. How many kids would you like, Charlie?'

She had a jumbled succession of mind pictures. Children running on Cranston's grassy slopes. Bikes and toys scattered on the sandstone terrace outside the lovely arched doors. Shrieks of laughter and daring as children swung on a rope into the creek. Talk about your life flashing before your eyes.

'Four,' Sam said, gazing fondly at her. 'What do you say, Charlie?'

'I say no.'

'Well, maybe four *is* overdoing it. Three, then——'

She clicked her tongue in exasperation. 'For heaven's sake—will you leave the subject alone? *No.*'

Sam sighed. 'Suppose I should have gone down on one knee and all that. You want me to say—love-you-forever and so on.' He wagged his finger. 'Can't say that, Charlie, darling—can't tell lies to you. Some women want lies. Not you.'

It was some kind of distinction, she supposed, wishing it took away the ache deep inside. She wouldn't block her ears if he told her the lie. She might even let herself believe it for a little while.

'You're ten years too late, Charlie. I've already played the fool in love and look where it got me.' He wagged a finger. 'No, no. Won't get suckered into that again. Now I just don't believe in—in——'

'Grand passions?' she said. 'Well, that's what I want, Sam. I want the grand passion. I want to be *important* to a man, not loved while I'm around and forgotten when I'm not. I want to be so important that his life won't be as good without me.' Charlotte paced around, warming to her definition. 'When I marry someone it'll be because anything else but being together is unthinkable—

not because we're great in bed or—or share common
interests. I don't want to—to be an audience to someone
whose life is complete without me. I want to be part of
the *act*!' She halted her pacing, gazed in frustration at
him. Sam was asleep. On reflection she thought it was
just as well. She called a cab and sat down until it arrived, indulging in the dubious pleasure of watching Sam
while he slept.

Two days later, when she went to his house to work on
the papers, Sam came home unexpectedly. It was a long
time since they'd discontinued the notes to each other
but, in spite of that, it was the first time that their
presence in the house had coincided since she'd caught
him in the bathtub. Charlotte heard him moving around
in the kitchen, heard his footsteps pass the door quickly
once, then a second time, slowing as if he might come
in. The third time, he opened the door.

'Good evening, Sam,' she said, relaxing a little. At
least he hadn't changed into that scandalous towelling
robe. Sam was, or had been, dressed for the office in
pin-striped trousers and matching waistcoat. Now his
shirt was open at the neck, sleeves rolled up, the knot
of his tie hung halfway down his chest.

'Hello, Charlie.' Sam turned side-on, leaned on the
door frame as he took a swallow from a can of beer.
Charlotte watched him narrowly. He looked uneasy. 'The
other night,' he said casually, watching the beer can as
he swirled the remaining liquid around. 'When I came
to your place——'

'Yes?'

'I'd had a few too many and I can't quite remember
what I—er——' Sam drank the last of the beer and
looked directly at her, with the air of a man facing up
to a firing squad. 'Did I ask you to marry me?'

Had he been worrying about this for the past two days?
Remembering the high-handed way he'd behaved over
Brian, she got some malicious enjoyment from the idea.

Brian had not been at all receptive to her apology, which meant a certain awkwardness in the staff-room. The score wasn't quite even yet, she decided. She smiled warmly at Sam. 'Yes, you did.'

His Adam's apple moved sharply in his throat. His pallor would have caused her some concern in other circumstances. It was funny to see a man like Sam so stricken, but it sparked off a cold rage in her too. 'When do we go shopping for the ring, Sam, darling?' She gave him an arch, proprietorial smile calculated to bring him out in a sweat. It did. Fascinated, she saw tiny beads of perspiration form on his forehead.

'Charlie,' he said in a harsh voice, 'I—er—don't know how to put this but—I didn't know what I was saying.'

She stared at him. 'I thought it was only rats that got you into that state,' she said, realising that she had vastly underestimated his fear of commitment. The bad years must have been worse than Sam had let on. 'Relax,' she said briskly, putting him out of his misery. 'Your proposal of marriage was purely hypothetical. "*If* I asked you, would you marry me?" were your actual words,' she said drily.

Colour flooded back into his face and he closed his eyes momentarily. She thought he might even be saying a little prayer of thanksgiving. All her sympathy departed. 'And my answer was no, anyway, so you can stop looking like a condemned man.'

Sam gave a huff of laughter, eyed her warmly. 'You're a girl in a million, Charlie.'

He did have a way of piling on the compensation prizes, she thought, closing the journal she was working on with a snap. She was as trustworthy as his mother, the one and only woman he'd ever truly liked as a friend, a girl in a million. She opened another journal and the musty smell of age and things past filled her nostrils. 'You should try to do something about that phobia of yours,' she said. He straightened, looked at her through narrowed eyes. Rather pugnaciously she added, 'You don't want to be terrified of rats all your life, do you?'

He went away laughing. What a girl in a million you are, Charlotte. You always leave them laughing.

The lull of autumn turned suddenly to winter. Sid, renewed after his brief bout of Outback busking, had done his stuff, and Martin's and Linda's new album was finished and being rushed through production. The Australian launch was planned for late August at a live benefit concert. By this time Gale had broken all her resolutions bar one. She had never borrowed another item belonging to Charlotte. Brian requested and was granted a transfer to another school and, in spite of his stuffiness, Charlotte missed him. She didn't like losing friends and resented Sam for precipitating this loss. First term exams loomed, and Charlotte knew some of her students would fail in spite of her efforts.

'I can't *stand* it when they fail, and I know they needn't have!' she said to Gale one cold, depressing night. 'Why on earth did I become a teacher?'

'You should be more detached. You care too much, that's your trouble,' Gale told her.

'Yes, Sam said that,' Charlotte muttered.

'Speaking of Sam, this was pushed under the door when I got home.' She tossed a plain envelope to Charlotte. 'No stamp on it. He must have delivered it himself.'

Charlotte's stupid flurry of reaction subsided when she saw the neatly printed 'Miss C. Wells' on the envelope. 'It's not from Sam——' She frowned. Shrugging, she opened the envelope. 'A money order—who on earth would be sending me a money order for twenty dollars?—Oh!' There was a note with it. '"Dear Miss Wells——"' Charlotte read the rest of it in silence.

'Who's it from?' Gale asked as Charlotte read it through a second time, her mouth silently forming the words. 'Why are you looking so funny?'

She thrust the pieces of paper at Gale, raised her hands in the air, then brought them together in a single clap. 'He kept the book!' she whispered. Laughing, she danced a little jig around the living-room.

'"Dear Miss Wells,"' Gale read out loud, '"Here is twenty dollars towards the cost of your tyres. I've got a job now but my wages aren't very good so it might be a while before I can pay it all back. Christopher Dunlop. P.S. It was an old copy of *Hamlet* that went up in smoke. I didn't burn the book you gave me." Well, well, the little creep's paying for the damage after all this time—so he should. But it's only twenty dollars, Charls. Nothing to *dance* about.'

Charlotte whirled around once more and came to a breathless stop, then dashed to the phone, dialled Sam's number.

'Sam,' she said, her voice bubbling with elation, 'he still has the book! He didn't burn the book!'

'Charlie—if this is about one of my forebears you like so much, surely it can wait——'

'Christopher Dunlop,' she cut in, rushing the words. 'It wasn't the book on bridges he burned in the school grounds that day, but an old copy of *Hamlet*, and I'm so glad.'

There was a short pause. 'Isn't that close to sacrilege, angel—an English teacher applauding the burning of the bard?'

She laughed. 'He paid me back some money towards the damage to my tyres—*Christopher*, paying me back! I thought when he left school that I'd lost him.'

'See, angel, you're the kind of person who just goes on making waves in a person's life, no matter how far away from you they run...or try to run.' It didn't altogether sound flattering. As if she were some kind of Nemesis, hounding people. Some of her exhilaration went. 'But don't get too excited. He might have tied a white flag to a stick, but he hasn't exactly surrendered yet.'

'It's not a question of his *surrendering*,' she said, disappointed by his reaction. 'It wasn't a contest of wills,
Sam. Anyway, I just had to tell you,' she said lamely.
'You're the only one who...well, I thought it was a
hopeful sign. He hasn't burned his bridges, so—who
knows?—one day he might even build one.'

'Maybe he'll name it after you, angel.'

His dry sarcasm hurt long after she'd hung up.
Charlotte couldn't fathom how a man who had so perfectly understood her feeling of failure with Christopher
should be unable to share her renewed hope. In spite of
everything, it was only the second time she'd felt truly
let down by Sam.

Cranston's roof structure had finally been rebuilt and
awaited the slate cladding. Doors were being made for
the lovely arched doorways, glass had been ordered for
the windows. The old stable building was being con-
verted into a caretaker's residence. Progress was watched
with almost proprietorial interest by Society members
who worked most weekends on the museum collection
in the coach house.

In August, when the peach tree by the creek was
showing the first signs of bud and the countryside was
ablaze with golden wattle, a storm swept in and tore off
a section of Cranston's newly laid roofing. The winds
whipped up a sheet of corrugated iron from the builders'
site and hurled it through one of the coach-house
windows. Broken glass and driving rain made a mess of
two exhibits and a freshly painted mural left to dry in
panels beneath the window. An urgent call for help went
out to clean up the mess and restore the items in time
for a heritage show a week distant.

Two days later, on Saturday, Charlotte drove to
Cranston. The rain that had fallen steadily since the
storm had eased for the moment and sunshine struck
glints from drying droplets on grass and trees. Cranston's
creek was a roaring torrent where it cut across the road

beneath the bridge that had been rebuilt twice. Charlotte
stopped the car to watch the swollen brown waters,
thinking of the same creek tranquilly winding around
flowering trees, rippled with pink blossom and white
shampoo bubbles. Sam, shiny with water, hands on hips,
naked as the day he was born, glowering at her. The lens
had been open and her finger had been on the shutter
button and she couldn't remember to this day, nearly a
year later, if she'd actually taken that picture. She would
never know.

Charlotte stepped on the accelerator and moments later
turned in at Cranston's new-old gates, snatched from a
demolition site in Parramatta. There was always a sense
of familiarity when she saw Cranston. It was, she knew,
something she was going to have to learn to live without.
Her research for Sam was coming to an end, and in six
months or less Cranston would no longer be a ruin. The
odd feeling of coming home was sheer illusion. There
was no place for her here.

As she slowed to park behind the other vehicles already
arrived, she saw how true that was. Sam was here and
there was a woman with him.

The girl was lovely, dashing in a shiny white trenchcoat
and boots and a man's snap-brimmed hat slanted over
one eye. She looked around as if she was waiting for
something—applause perhaps? Charlotte was conscious
that she herself looked drab and businesslike in denims,
tartan shirt and boots. Sam looked over as Charlotte got
out of her car. There was something challenging about
him that reminded her of someone, she couldn't think
who. She gave a carefree little wave and a smile broad
enough to be seen from that distance and moved off
towards the coach house.

'Charlie. *Charlie!*' a peremptory voice called. 'Look
at me! Did you bring your camera?' It was Stevie. The
sight of him was a double blow to the solar plexus. So
it was a family threesome. Surely Sam wouldn't bring
just any girl to Cranston, with his son. She must be

special. The old familiar feeling of exclusion swept over
her, stronger than ever. Quickly she pinned on her smile
as a bicycle sped towards her, bell trilling. Stevie wore
a bright yellow raincoat and black rubber boots. 'See—
I'm riding all by myself now.' Proudly he displayed the
absence of training wheels and invited her to take photographs of this phenomenon.

Sam came over with his companion. 'Belinda, this is
Charlie.'

Belinda frowned down at her boot. 'Oh, hi,' she said
with a vague smile, and grabbed Sam's arm to steady
herself as she raised her foot and peered backwards at
her heel. 'Are you the one who was buried alive in the
cellar with Sam? It must have been awful. I'd go to pieces
if I was locked in somewhere in the dark. I've got a
phobia about dark, closed-in places.'

Belinda wobbled on one foot and Sam put his arm
around her waist. Her hands scrabbled at him, her bright
red fingernails flashing like Christmas tree lights before
she got a grip on his shirtfront. Once she was steady
again, bolstered by Sam's strong arm, she concentrated
on flicking mud from her boot. Her casual response to
Sam's proximity seemed to indicate familiarity. She
looked up and beamed at him, a hazy, dreamy look in
her eyes. 'Thanks,' she said, and shared the smile around
unstintingly. Sam looked at Charlotte with an odd expression and that too reminded her of something or
someone. The connection escaped her as she strove for
the pleasant, platonic smile the occasion demanded.

'Nice to meet you. Excuse me,' Charlotte said pol-
itely. 'I must get to work.'

In the coach-house she was quickly deployed by Mrs
Humphries to pick glass fragments out of the mural
surface. Charlotte spent an hour doing so, then began
the job of disguising the pock-marked surface with filler.
Stevie wandered through now and then asking Charlotte
questions and demanding her services as a photographer
until she felt quite irritable with him.

'Won't your father and Belinda be looking for you?'

'Daddy's inside on a ladder, looking at the walls with another man. Belinda said I could come in here if I wanted.'

Belinda didn't mind shoving off the job as baby-sitter, Charlotte thought savagely. Stevie ferreted around, picking up bits and pieces and talking to the others. Mrs Fulbright and Mrs Humphries made a fuss of him. She saw him wander off again carrying a glass jar and made a mental note to warn him against running with it when he came back.

Stevie didn't come back. It was twenty minutes before she realised she hadn't caught even a glimpse of him. The glass jar nagged at her conscience. If he took it with him on the bike and fell with it... 'Has anyone seen Stevie?' she asked around casually. No one had. Of course, Sam might have taken him home by now. That was a logical assumption, for the weather had taken a turn for the worse. The sun struggled to make a showing as clouds scudded in on a wind that whistled through the broken coach house window, impeding a member's valiant attempts to reglaze it.

Sam's car was still there. She went to check the builders' piles of loam and sand, a favourite playground of Stevie's. Covering sheets of iron, held down with bricks, flapped madly making hollow, musical bellows. There were bike tracks all around but no sign of Stevie. 'Stevie,' she called, listening for the sound of a bicycle bell. She looked into the partly restored stables and made her way across to the big house. Stevie's bike lay on the stone terrace, the wheels turning slightly in the wind. For no defined reason, Charlotte began to feel anxious.

Belinda was seated on a cushion on the front steps, a picnic hamper open beside her. She held a wine glass and looked rather forlorn. In the hand that held her hat on was a half-eaten chicken leg.

'Have you seen Stevie?' Charlotte asked.

Belinda looked all around vaguely. 'He was here a minute ago. He'll be around somewhere,' she said, filling a second wine glass. 'He's probably gone inside. Sam's upstairs trying to cover something up in case it rains again. Oh, shivers,' she said as she spilled the wine. 'I'm taking Sam a glass of wine. Help yourself.'

Charlotte, unable to pin her escalating anxiety on to anything concrete, stood irresolute. She cupped her hands to her mouth and called, 'Stevie!' Her voice was picked up by a gust of wind and carried away. Something nagged at her. Something that had triggered off this apprehension. Slowly she went down the steps past the opened hamper and the bottle of wine.

Bottle. Stevie with a glass jar. She should have warned him against running with it in case he fell and the glass shattered. No, that was a worry but that wasn't what bothered her. It was something else. But what?

The images came suddenly. Stevie with another glass jar on another day when the sun shone and the cicadas droned... Stevie, collecting tadpoles in the creek, scooping them up in a jar. 'In a jar—in the creek——' The water had been a mere trickle then, after months of dry weather, but now... 'Oh, my God,' she whispered, thinking of the torrent she'd seen under the bridge. Filled with dread, she began to run. 'Stevie!' she yelled in a long-drawn-out cry as she went, faster and faster down the undulating slope to the creek. 'Ste-vie!'

CHAPTER ELEVEN

UPSTAIRS beneath the bare new roof rafters, Sam battled with a tarpaulin. The wind got underneath, ballooned it and he was almost dragged off his feet. Sam cursed roundly. It must be another storm coming. At first he paid no heed to the thin thread of sound hidden in the billows of sound. Every part of the house that was remotely loose, rattled and flapped and banged.

'Stop and have a drink, Sam,' Belinda called from under some of the original roof cover. She raised the wine glass and gave her lovely smile, and Sam forbore to point out the difficulties of drinking champagne with both hands full of tarpaulin.

'Where's Stevie?' he asked.

'He went over to the coach-house and must have wandered off to play. Your friend Charlie is rounding him up.'

The thin sound was repeated again, like the distant, anguished cry of a bird. The hairs on his neck rose. 'Rounding him up? You make him sound like a herd of sheep. Where is she looking for him?' Again that sound. Stevie. It was Charlie calling his son's name and there was something in it...he let the tarpaulin go and the wind snatched greedily at it. In two strides he had a grip on Belinda's arm and was moving her to the stairs. 'Which way did she go?'

'You're spilling the wine——' Belinda said, startled.

Sam let out an expletive, shook her arm and the last of the wine slopped over Belinda's boots. 'Which way?'

'Oh, shivers,' Belinda wailed, looking down at her boots. 'I *think* she was going down that slope.'

'Towards the creek?' Sam's blood ran cold. 'No, he wouldn't go down there—I told him it was out of bounds.

167

Go and tell Mrs Fulbright and the others to look for
him——' He took the stairs two at a time. Outside, the
wind howled behind him one moment, buffeted him
backwards the next as he ran down the slippery slope,
his mind feeding on visions of rushing, muddied water.
'Tadpoles grow into frogs, Daddy,' Stevie's voice piped
in his head. He'd been talking about frogs on the way
here. Shouldn't have brought him out here. Should have
left him with Mrs Hume. Sam stumbled, fell and rolled.
Panting, he picked himself up. He was going to feel an
idiot about this, he thought, when he went back and
found his son tucking into his lunch. Charlie had
probably found Stevie looking at a bird's nest fallen from
a tree or something. She was probably giving him a long
lecture about the environment. 'One day I'm going to
catch a tadpole and keep it until it turns into a frog...'

Catch a tadpole. And the creek was breaking its banks.
Sam crashed through the undergrowth, fear anaesthe-
tising him against the scratch and scrape of thorns and
branches. The shrubbery dumped last night's raindrops
on him. 'Stevie—Charlie——' he yelled, knuckling the
water from his eyes to be confronted with the torrent of
brownish yellow water. 'Oh, my God——' Frantically
he bellowed their names again, searching along the edges
of the water and this time there was an answer. A treble
voice shaking with fear. 'Daddy, Daddy!' Sam saw the
bright yellow raincoat first, then the small bobbing head
close in to the nearest bank but caught in the current.
'I'm coming, Stevie——' he yelled, and crashed along
the bank level with his son, shedding his jacket as he
went, his mind clearing with action. He plunged into the
water, bracing himself against the current, and that was
when he saw Charlie.

She was further down from Stevie, being dragged
faster as the current boiled around a built-up snag of
tree trunks and debris. Her face turned towards him once
and she saw him. Her eyes opened wide and she moved
her mouth in words he could see but couldn't hear.

'Sam,' she cried, and, 'Stevie.' He saw it all in split seconds before the current took her under. The last of Charlie to disappear was her hand, pointing at Stevie.

'Ah—no! Charlie! Stevie!' Sam's roar of pain bellowed above the roar of wind and water. Tears poured down his face as he threw himself into the water in an agony of indecision. Both of them needed him. Which one needed him most? What if he rescued one and couldn't make it to the other? 'Don't do this to me,' he implored a higher power. Sam had a feeling of his life shattering, everything he'd thought important fading away. If anything happened to either of them... Sam ploughed through the water, striking bargains for their safety, making promises.

'Daddy, Daddy!'

He dashed water from his eyes and followed the voice.

Stevie had been swept sideways on to a log that had been washed partly on to shore. Gasping, the little boy hauled himself along it, his bright yellow raincoat in tatters, and fell into the bushes. His head reappeared a moment later. 'Daddy,' he bawled, knuckling his eyes.

'Move back to that tree, Stevie. Hold on to it and don't move from there. Promise me you won't move, Stevie! I have to get Charlie.'

The little boy sobbed and gulped but obeyed. 'I promise,' he said.

Charlotte was gone. Desperately he searched the roiling surface. 'Charlie—where the hell are you? Don't you bloody dare drown—*Charlie*! You can't leave me, dammit!'

He saw the flash of tartan for a split second and battled towards it. Lungs bursting, muscles on fire, he fought towards it, came close enough to grab the tartan fabric next time it appeared. His hand closed on Charlie's shirt and he saw there was no movement from her, not even a feeble one, and his mind reeled away from it. Silently he recited the Lord's Prayer like a child again, over and over. She was limp, cold, and he seized her, clasped her slim body as if his life depended on it, not just hers, and struggled to the bank.

He hauled Charlotte out of the water some twenty yards downstream from the place he'd left his son. She wasn't breathing, her heart wasn't beating. 'Charlie—come on.' He opened her mouth, checked for obstructions with shaking fingers and breathed into her. 'Come on, you gabby, lecturing, smarty-pants teacher,' he growled, ripped aside the tartan shirt and pressed sharply over her heart. How many of these should he do between the mouth-to-mouth? All those first-aid posters in all those locker-rooms. Why the hell hadn't he taken more notice? He gave her another breath, pounded at her chest. 'Come on!' he yelled. 'How the hell are the Christopher Dunlops of the world going to build any bridges without you to badger them? Breathe, dammit, Charlie!'

And on the third borrowed breath she coughed. It was the sweetest sound he'd ever heard. Gently he lifted her, clasped her to him, rocking as she choked and wheezed her way back to life.

Only then did he notice that some of the others were there. One of the men carried a sobbing Stevie over to Sam.

'Stevie?' Charlotte croaked.

'He's safe,' Sam told her, an arm around each of them. Their cold, soft faces pressed close each side of him and he gripped them tight as if the water might rise up yet and take them from him.

'Thank God,' he whispered. 'I never want to have to choose between you again.'

Charlotte felt life flow back into her. Sam's arm was hard around her and his cheek pressed against hers and in spite of the chill of his skin, she took warmth from him. Sam was saying something but she couldn't catch the words over the tumult of the creek and Stevie's sobs and the ragged gasp of her own breathing.

'My dear Charlotte,' Mrs Fulbright said, hurrying to her side. 'How dreadful. Thank goodness Sam knew how to revive you—we must get you dry, quickly, all of you. And something hot to drink. Dot, send someone up to put the kettle on. And bring down those picnic rugs——'

Helping hands separated Charlotte from Sam.

'Take Charlie to a doctor,' Sam said to Mrs Fulbright. 'No heartbeat. Have to be checked out. Ring me, let me know.' Charlotte looked over at him. He wore the strangest expression, as if he expected her to say something. No heartbeat? She'd been dead and he revived her. Charlotte's hand went to her chest. Her heart gave a bump as if it might fail her again. 'Thank you, Sam,' she said hoarsely. But that wasn't what he was waiting for. Sam continued to stare at her over Stevie's head, his blue eyes shocked and vulnerable as she'd never seen them. It was as if Sam's usual disguises had been swept away in the flooded creek and left him naked. For a moment she thought she saw everything she'd ever wanted there in his eyes, and her drowned spirit soared. But she was assisted inexorably away from Sam, and Belinda was there in her shiny white raincoat and Sam turned towards her like a man in a dream. The trouble with wanting to believe in something, she thought, was that you could always interpret things to suit. Sam cared about her, of course. He'd just saved her life, hadn't he? But he was shocked that he'd come so close to losing his son. That was what had put that look in Sam's eyes. He turned away, comforting Stevie who clung like a limpet.

Charlotte was carried up the slope by two Society members, supervised by Fiona Fulbright. She was wrapped in a picnic blanket produced from the boot of Mrs Humphries' car, given hot tea with lashings of sugar and driven to see a doctor, who insisted she remain for an hour before he let her go home. Mrs Fulbright had driven Charlotte's car home, Mrs Humphries told her.

Charlotte hadn't even thought to ask about her car. In her passivity and confusion she hadn't even said goodbye to Stevie or Sam.

Mrs Fulbright and Mrs Humphries were kind and concerned and Charlotte thought they would never go. 'Straight to bed,' Mrs Fulbright advised as they left at last. 'You were very brave, my dear, going in after little Stevie like that.'

'Very brave,' Mrs Humphries said. 'I think we should bring the matter up at a future meeting, don't you, Fiona?'

'I didn't rescue anyone. I had to be rescued myself,' Charlotte felt impelled to point out.

'Nevertheless.' Mrs Fulbright gave a little nod of determination which turned the single word into a sentence.

After she'd closed the door, Charlotte leaned against it. Weakly she giggled. Was she to be the Society's heroine? Would they strike a medal for her? Would she be raised on the Agenda under 'general business'? The giggle turned to laughter and as quickly to tears. Desolation struck through to her soul. She realised now that, in the very heart of her, she had never quite stopped hoping that Sam might one day love her. He cared about her, and she'd always had trouble giving up on people who cared. The cessation of the hope, unlike that time in the cellar, brought no relief. It brought a terrible bleakness that stretched out before her like an endless winter. Wrapping her arms around herself, she slumped against the door, lonely as she'd never been before.

Gale was out. The rooms of the flat were empty and unloving. Without conscious thought she went to the phone and dialled the number of her parents' city apartment. They might be home. After a few clicks, she heard her father's voice in a recorded message. ' . . . if you care to leave a message and phone number after the beeps, we'll get back to you.' She choked back a laugh. She waited for the beeps and said, steadily enough, 'Hi. It's Charlotte. I'll see you at the concert on Friday.' Then she played an Earthbound record for the sound of their voices. If she scoured the evening sports programmes on television, she might even catch one of Sam's recorded interviews. All the people she loved, available at the push of a button. She turned everything off and went to bed.

She found the nerve after all and wore the strapless black dress to her parents' concert at the Opera House. People turned to look at her and she enjoyed the sensation. Afterwards, as she waited her chance to speak to Martin and Linda who were mingling with the patrons she caught the eye of Earthbound's sultry drummer. Quinn had only ever made dutiful conversation with her before, but tonight he came over and gave her the full, smouldering treatment that earned him a fan-following all his own, and said, 'Off the planet, baby.'

She managed not to laugh or take his admiration seriously. Any moment now, he would drift away again. Concentration spans were short in the music industry. But Quinn stayed longer than she expected, wolfishly paying tribute to the efforts of Gale and a cosmetician called Moira. Gale had had her wish and crimped Charlotte's fair hair out of its normal limp straightness into an unexpected blonde cloud.

'Honestly, it'll change your life,' Gale had said as she crimped. She had studied Charlotte's faraway face. 'Or is it too late for that?'

At a department store counter, Moira had laid out a palette of colours to challenge Charlotte's pastel soul. Plums and silver for eyes, bronze for cheeks, deep Venetian red for mouth. Only when the result was teamed with the black dress had Charlotte realised Moira's genius.

'Stun-ning,' Quinn said.

It was good for her ego, but she tired of Quinn long before he tired of her, which was something of a turn-around. She tried to attract her parents' attention but they were surrounded. For a time she stood and watched

them, thinking that their oneness on stage was not merely
show-business. Their bodies turned naturally one towards
the other. Their eyes met, smiled, moved on. Their hands
touched in passing as if to say, I'm with you. Sharing
their energy. The bond between them had to be strong
to let them stay happy in an industry full of discontent
and insecurity. Funny. She didn't want to love anyone
like her parents. But she wanted a partnership very much
like theirs. No wonder she was sometimes jealous of
them.

In the end she left a note for them with Gale, who
was in her element gathering autographs, and slipped
away at half-past midnight to take a taxi home. Not quite
Cinderella, she thought, feeling a dull lethargy steal over
her.

A black BMW was parked outside the apartments.
Charlotte snapped upright, heart racing, all systems go.
There were thousands of black BMWs. The cab head-
lights swept across the front of the apartment building
and the man who leaned there by the door, waiting. A
big man. There were hundreds of big men, she told
herself. This one had very broad shoulders, but there
were dozens of big men with broad shoulders. Adrenalin
pounded through her body as she paid the driver and
began to walk along the path. Light spilled out from the
apartment building foyer silhouetting him, highlighting
darkest brown hair and a familiar arrogant tilt of the
head. Only one Sam.

A wave of euphoria hit her but she struggled out from
under. There would be a good reason for this visit, she
thought sourly, remembering the time he'd called to see
her when Ruth got married again. He probably wanted
her to resume work on his family papers, or wanted her
advice as a teacher regarding Stevie, or simply some tea
and sympathy from good old Charlie. Briskly, she walked
up to him.

He stared, straightened from the waiting pose as she
came into the light. Shadows defined the strong bones

of his face, heightened the raised eyebrow illusion of the scar, making him look as if he frowned and smiled at the same time. 'Charlie——?' His eyes roamed over her hair, her bare, pale shoulders and the strapless black that swathed her body to the hips then split to show her legs. She felt buoyed up enough by Quinn's admiration earlier to do a slow pirouette to show off the dress.

'You owe me twenty bucks,' she said.

He laughed and she was suddenly furious. Just when she was doing so well, he had to turn up and ruin everything. How was she supposed to forget a man whose most casual appearance could send her reeling for cover? Damn him. 'I'm tired, Sam. What did you want?'

She jabbed her key in the lock and opened the foyer door, turned ready to close it on him. But Sam walked past, crowding her so that she stepped back. He shoved his hands in his pockets and looked down at her. 'You,' he said, with a faint, tense smile.

She suffered a small relapse at that, but anger saved her. The door slammed and her high heels clicked out her disapproval as she crossed the tiled floor. 'Well, you can't have me,' she said, not looking back to see if he followed her up the stairs. The black dress frou-froued frivolously, undermining the mood she wanted to create, and she held on to the skirt, trying to stop the sound.

He muttered something under his breath and came after her, catching up two steps at a time. 'Charlie—that day at the creek——'

She stopped and looked at him. 'Was Stevie all right? Did he have nightmares?'

'Only the first night. He wouldn't let me out of his sight initially but he bounced back. It's me who's still having nightmares,' he added.

'I'm sorry to hear that.' Charlotte went up another flight of stairs and along the corridor to her apartment door.

'I come out in a cold sweat every time I think what might have happened,' he said, watching her find another key and rattle it in the lock. 'I shake all over.'

'Sounds like flu,' she said, opening the door. He must have thought there was a fair chance she would slam it, because he laid a hand flat against it and scowled at her. She thought she heard him say something about Christopher.

'What? Did you say Christopher Dunlop?'

'Yes!' Sam glared. 'There's no getting away from you, Charlie. Dammit, that kid and I did our best. OK! I surrender. I want you. I need you. I love you. Marry me.'

Tides of hope came rushing in to drown her again. Charlotte fought to keep her head up. 'Damn you, Sam! Are you drunk again? I told you before, I won't marry you to be another "safe harbour". I won't marry you to provide you with more children to play with when you can't have Stevie. I won't be second-best—I don't want to be an audience, I want to be——'

'Part of the act,' he finished. 'I know. You must have told me before. Just shut up and *listen*!' he said when she started to speak. 'I've always thought I'd rather spend a year in a cellar full of rats than get married again.'

Charlotte snorted. 'A cellar full of rats! What a poet you are!' Rather desperately she jiggled the key from the lock. Sam's hand descended heavily on her shoulder and he turned her to face him.

'I made mistakes and got my insides ripped out and I vowed I'd never risk that again,' he said in a low voice. 'I thought I could persuade you to live with me—no strings, just fun—and I was glad in the end when you refused because, once I got over the euphoria of being alive again, I got scared.' He let the statement stand alone for a moment as if it were a confession to be noted. 'Being a sucker for punishment, of course, I couldn't leave well enough alone. I had to get you in to work at

my house!' He gave a hoot at his own idiocy. 'I should
have run like the devil, but I didn't and now I've run
out of steam.'

'I don't appreciate your metaphors,' she said tartly.
'You make me sound like some pursuing harpy, and let
me tell you that at no time did I ever pursue——'

Sam rolled his eyes. 'I propose marriage and she cri-
ticises my metaphors! Will you stop being an English
teacher for a minute? For Pete's sake,' he added irritably, 'why am I spilling out my guts in a corridor?'
With one of those lightning turns of speed he was famous
for, he pushed her inside, closed the door. Purposefully
he plucked the keys from her hand and hitched an arm
around her, gathering her in urgently, turning his face
into the curve of her neck. His chest rose and fell as he
sighed and held her tightly to him a moment longer, not
kissing her, nothing but that fast, needy embrace. Then
abruptly he let go.

Charlotte stayed there, her back to the door literally
and metaphorically, heart pounding so violently that she
put her hands to her chest to check that the strapless
black hadn't fallen down. Sam tossed the keys into a
chair then stuck his hands in his pockets. He took them
out again almost at once, smoothed his hair, shifted the
knot of his tie as if it was too tight. Fascinated, she
watched the series of nervous moves, hardly daring to
make anything of it.

At last he said, huskily, 'It was the worst day of my
life, Charlie, seeing you and Stevie in danger—the two
people in the world I most——' he stopped for a
moment, reaching for the word '—treasure.'

Silence. The kitchen clock ticked and the videotape
whirred, recording a late-night horror movie for Gale.
Charlotte stared at Sam. Treasure. An odd choice of
word for Sam, a beautiful word that confounded her
and brought with it the first wave of warmth she'd felt
this past wintry week. 'Charlie—you know how much
Stevie means to me. If I lost him I'd feel as if there was

no meaning in my life. He's part of me.' He let his head
tilt back and closed his eyes briefly. 'When I saw you
and Stevie—I didn't know which one of you to go to
first. I couldn't bear to lose either of you.'

She'd thought once that, if he ever loved a woman
half as much as he loved his son, that woman would be
luckier than most. Charlotte remembered Sam holding
her and Stevie and saying something she didn't hear. She
remembered his shock, his eyes wide and undefended
and telling her what she'd wanted to believe for a long
time and, ironically, hadn't been able to at the moment
of truth. The shock was gone, but the rest of it was there
in his eyes, so blue and serious. Sam really did love her.
She thought bells were ringing somewhere, but there were
no chimes here.

'You saved my life,' she said huskily.

'I saved mine.' He reached out, touched her hair. 'I
love you, Charlie. I hope to God you love me too.'

'You,' she said huskily. 'And Stevie.'

'You, me and Stevie,' Sam said, relishing the sound
of it.

'We'll make a great team.'

He grinned. 'You know, it would have saved a whole
lot of time and trouble if I'd told you I loved you when
we were rescued from the cellar.'

Her eyes opened wide. 'But you didn't love me then.'
That he loved her at all was suddenly, marvellously
definite, cast in stone, as if she'd always known, yet
somehow it was brand new, too.

'Didn't—recognise it then,' Sam grunted. 'I thought
you were soft-hearted and brave and a pain in the neck.
You were the first woman I ever met who was fair and
straight from the shoulder. Almost one of the boys, in
fact.' His eyes dropped down to the swell of her breasts
sculpted in the strapless black and he grinned. He
brushed her shoulder with the backs of his fingers, bent
and kissed her bare skin. Charlotte's breathing
quickened. Darling Sam. He didn't know what he was

doing to her. 'I didn't want to recognise how I felt because I didn't want to get involved, but you were under my skin like—a burr under a sock,' he went on, 'The most confusing woman. I felt irritated, protective. I wanted you.'

'Well, I knew *that*,' she said, leaning back against the door as Sam's big hands met around her waist. A burr under a sock, she thought dreamily. The man was definitely a romantic.

'I needed you.' He brooded over the unfamiliar words a bit, staying at arm's length. Considering the length of Sam's arms, it was a fair distance. 'It was why I—didn't tell you I was still technically married.' Charlotte stiffened a bit.

'You were a rat, Sam.'

He winced. 'I just thought somehow you already knew there was no divorce as such—and when I realised you didn't, well, hell, Charlie, it was a bit late for me. You'd kissed me and made me feel, I don't know—optimistic, strong in the middle of disaster—I wanted to go on feeling like that. I needed you.'

'You said "wanted" before.'

'That too. But it isn't only a woman who likes to be held, Charlie, in bad times. It wasn't just a sexual thing— it was——' He cast around for the word. 'Comfort. Peace.'

She glowed. Sam certainly was coming up with some fantastic words tonight. Words that wouldn't have been in his vocabulary a year ago. Her outrage, she thought, had been more at the feeling of being tricked than anything. His marriage had been a leftover technicality, his wife already gone from him. And Sam's evasion hadn't been one of the petty manipulations she hated.

'In that case,' she said, smiling, 'I can live with it.'

He held her there at arm's length, just looking at her, stoking up the fires. 'I really didn't think you'd buy it,' he said, of the strapless black.

'You still owe me twenty bucks,' she reminded him. 'Put your money where your mouth is, Sam.'

Laughing, he felt in his pocket, drew out a note and tucked it into the strapless bodice. His fingers were warm against her skin, the note crackled as he pushed it well down between her breasts.

'Paid in full,' he said, and pulled her slowly towards him. For a fast man he could be slow so divinely. Sam Buchanan in slow motion was a memorable experience, all the sports commentators said so. She watched his face drawing nearer, saw the love in his eyes deepen, felt his embrace even before his arms went around her.

'Charlie,' he murmured close in her ear, 'marry me?'

'What if I said no?' she said, sliding her arms around his neck.

He groaned. 'Then I'd have to go to Plan B.'

'What's Plan B?'

'A lot more grovelling, bended knee, flowers every day, love poems——'

'You—writing love poems?' She winced. 'In that case I'll accept on Plan A.' Charlotte looked at him, suddenly deserted by ready words and humour as she saw his tension. She held his face in her hands and said, seriously, 'I love you, Sam. I want to marry you.'

'Ah.' He kissed her impatiently, lifting her up on to her toes, warming her bare back with his hands. Sam in slow motion, or Sam at full speed—he took her breath away. She couldn't decide which she liked best. Wrapped in his arms, she thought she would never have to.

He took her hand. 'Come on, let's go before your cousin comes home.' The door closed and they went down the stairs, Charlotte's dress, unchecked, frou-frouing frivolously.

'Wait a minute.' She stopped on the stairs. 'What about Belinda? Is she—were you—I mean, the two of you——?'

'She isn't, we weren't—there is no "two of us".'

'That's not how it looked. She looked crazy about you.'

'Belinda looks crazy about everyone. She's blind as a bat without her glasses—short-sighted. Didn't you notice? It gives her the misty-eyed look that earns her bread and butter.' Sam took her arm but Charlotte resisted. 'She's a model, Charlie. Under contract to do some work for Champions. The only thing Belinda was interested in that day was how she looked and if the photographer would come to get some pictures of her draped against some dead trees. The light wasn't good enough, so he didn't come.'

'You introduced her as if she was—a personal friend.'

Sam scratched his nose. 'Yeah. Well, I was making one last stand, wasn't I? Trying to convince myself that I wasn't crazy about you. Belinda was all over me like a rash, using me as a prop, and I could see what you thought and I pushed it a bit further, that's all.' He shook his head in self-deprecation. 'But I was only pretending to burn my bridges. Like Christopher Dunlop. He knew life would never be the same again because of Miss Wells and so did I—when I saw you in your tartan shirt and your schoolmarm hairdo. But we put up a fight, Chris and I. It took a flood to stop me kidding myself.'

Maybe his expression that day had reminded her of Christopher's the day he burned his book. 'Put up a *fight*?' she complained. 'Making a *last stand*. Must you use warlike language? We're talking about falling in love, aren't we?'

'But I didn't want to fall in love—so it *was* war for me, Charlie.'

She was thoughtful while he opened the car door for her.

'Maybe you feel you've lost the war, then,' she said, anxiety creasing her brow.

Sam rubbed the frown-line with his thumb. 'This is one war you win when you lose,' he said softly, and

smiled down at her like a victor. 'Get in, Charlie. We're
going to my place.'

Definitely a victor. Her anxiety vanished.

'I don't recall a schoolmarm hairdo,' she said severely.

'I find I'm getting to like it,' he said, reaching over
to touch the soft clouds of crimped hair. 'I like it any
way at all.'

'Even sopping wet—in rats' tails?'

He shuddered. 'Must you keep talking about rats?'

'One phobia down, one to go.' She giggled.

His house was perfect, tidy, waiting to be lived in. He
put on a light and drew her along to the one room she
had never seen in his house.

He sat on his king-sized bed and pulled her on to his
lap in one of those flashes of speed that Sam was famous
for. It was followed by some splendid slow motion.

'I had the most terrible bruises the day after you pulled
me out of the creek,' she said, kissing his neck.

'Had to restart your heart. After all, you restarted
mine.'

'And you revived me.'

'Mouth to mouth.'

'The kiss of life.' Sam demonstrated the technique.
He inched down the zip-fastener on the black dress, then
bent and brushed his mouth over her bare shoulder and
down into the hollow between her breasts. The twenty-
dollar note crackled.

'Putting my mouth where my money is,' he said.

Haunting Old Houses was launched at the end of
summer. Suitably, the occasion took place in Cranston,
to which a chapter in the book was devoted. Of all the
lovely buildings captured there, it was the only one still
surviving. Scaffolding still spiked around part of it, interior walls awaited some loving care but some of it—
the drawing-room and the kitchen, and the stunning entrance and staircase—was fully restored. Not that it was
furnished in the style of the original period. Quite the

contrary. Sam liked modern furniture, and the high-ceilinged rooms with their elaborately moulded cornices made the perfect foil for the uncluttered lines of leather chairs and glass tables. 'My ancestors were good on buildings but their furniture is too damned uncomfortable,' Sam said. 'Take the best from the past and add the best from the present, that makes sense to me.' Charlotte had no argument with that. Only the main bedroom was entirely in period right down to the handmade quilt on the bed. 'Tom, Dick and Harry would have appreciated today's mattress technology, though,' Sam remarked as he tested the springing.

Guests, shown through Cranston, expressed surprise at the atmosphere of warmth even in those vast, bare rooms with peeling walls and creaking floorboards. 'It doesn't seem as *cold* as most old places,' Charlotte's publisher said.

'You haven't tried the cellar.'

The Marshall brothers were there in their best shiny suits and Paisley ties. The restored Cranston was really something, they agreed. But Ross and Barry eyed the house wistfully and also agreed that she would have been a beauty to bring down, a sentiment that won some stiff disapproval from Mrs Fulbright and Mrs Humphries.

Speeches were made, cocktails were consumed, applause rose and was lost in the soaring vestibule. Gale gave her considered opinion that the book was better than she'd expected and that Sam was out of this world. There was a boyish quality to his smile and a new, contented look in his eyes. With his broad shoulders improving the drape of a superb navy blazer, Sam was a splendid sight. Gale sighed and said in Charlotte's ear, 'You do make it hard for a person to keep a promise.'

'What promise?'

'Never, ever to borrow anything of yours.' She giggled. 'The house isn't bad, either. Not bad for an old dump. Plenty of room for all that jumping around.'

Sam's attention was caught. 'What jumping around is that?'

'She started it out of the blue,' Gale said. 'Not long after you'd been stuck in the cellar here, actually. Calisthenics.'

Sam grinned. 'Calisthenics—is that so? What made you start that, angel?' he said with malicious pleasure.

'Come to think of it, she hasn't been doing it lately,' Gale said. 'Not since you got engaged.'

'You don't know how pleased I am to hear that,' Sam said with his blandest smile.

Charlotte gave him a repressive classroom stare, then obediently turned to have her photograph taken. A television cameraman had been and gone already and another had just arrived. The story of Cranston's revival, the cellar incident and the subsequent engagement of Sam and Charlotte had earned *Haunting Old Houses* more than its share of initial interest.

Her parents had sent a note to say they wouldn't come. Charlotte had been certain they would. To be photographed in such a beautiful old place, launching their daughter's book, toasting their famous son-in-law to be—she would have thought Martin and Linda would jump at it. She had imagined them sweeping in, taking centre stage quite naturally. The stars. Puzzled, she had read and re-read their note.

'We'll be with you in spirit, Charlotte, but we won't come. It's your day. Love your book. Martin and Linda.'

'*Won't* come,' she said to Sam. 'Not can't come.'

'Letting you have the limelight?' he suggested. 'You know what it would be like if they came. Maybe this is their equivalent to the home-made cake for the cake stall, hmm?'

Charlotte laughed. Maybe it was.

It was almost dusk when the last guest started down the drive to disappear into the rose-gold haze of sun and dust. Arm in arm, Charlotte and Sam walked through

the crabbed old apple trees that Richard had planted in
his third attempt to grow something.

'Maybe we should try grapevines again,' Sam said.

'Are you serious?'

'Been thinking about it ever since you showed me that
old bottle label. Wine from the Cranston Estate. There's
a vineyard not far from here that makes very good
Chardonnay. I know nothing about it. Can you see me
as a winemaker?'

She smiled. 'As anything you want to be.'

Sam took her hand. 'Come. I want to show you something before the light fails.'

He guided her down to the creek where the weeds and
thorny undergrowth had been trimmed and the trees,
planted so long ago, stood free of tangles. Charlotte
stopped to run her fingers over the inscription. '"Robert
and Emma. Met by chance Wednesday, 26th June,
1839",' she said out loud. 'I wonder how they met? I
wonder who they were.'

Sam bent and picked up something from the grass. A
hammer and chisel.

'What are you doing?'

'Carrying on the tradition,' he said, drawing her a little
to the side. 'I know how fond you are of traditions.'

There were new marks on the same tree. Her eyes
opened wide as she saw that he had been working on
this for some time. 'Sam and Charlotte,' he had carved.

'You put your name first,' she accused.

'Of course. So did Bob. I don't mess with tradition.'

Sam and Charlotte. 'It looks nice,' she said with a
lump in her throat.

She watched him carve the date of their first meeting.
If her sense of direction had been better, she might have
taken the proper fork in the track and gone direct to
Cranston. She might never have met Sam, never been
trapped in the cellar. Might have taken her photographs,
had her sandwiches and wine under a shady tree and
gone back to her nice, neat life not knowing that this

marvellous man was here, so close. Met by chance. The
late afternoon sun filtered through the leaves and lay
pale gold on the old inscription and the new.

'There, how's that?' Sam laid down his tools and stood
back to admire his work.

'I love it,' she said and read out loud. 'Sam and
Charlotte met here by chance, Friday 13th——' She
laughed and wrapped her arms around his neck.
'Thirteen,' she said, kissing him. 'My lucky number.'

Next Month's Romances

Each month you can choose from a world of variety in romance with Mills & Boon. Below are the new titles to look out for next month, why not ask either Mills & Boon Reader Service or your Newsagent to reserve you a copy of the titles you want to buy — just tick the titles you would like to order and either post to Reader Service or take it to any Newsagent and ask them to order your books.

Please save me the following titles:		Please tick	√
STORMFIRE	Helen Bianchin		
LAW OF ATTRACTION	Penny Jordan		
DANGEROUS SANCTUARY	Anne Mather		
ROMANTIC ENCOUNTER	Betty Neels		
A DARING PROPOSITION	Miranda Lee		
NO PROVOCATION	Sophie Weston		
LAST OF THE GREAT FRENCH LOVERS	Sarah Holland		
CAVE OF FIRE	Rebecca King		
NO MISTRESS BUT LOVE	Kate Proctor		
INTRIGUE	Margaret Mayo		
ONE LOVE FOREVER	Barbara McMahon		
DOUBLE FIRE	Mary Lyons		
STONE ANGEL	Helen Brooks		
THE ORCHARD KING	Miriam Macgregor		
LAW OF THE CIRCLE	Rosalie Ash		
THE HOUSE ON CHARTRES STREET	Rosemary Hammond		

If you would like to order these books from Mills & Boon Reader Service please send £1.70 per title to: Mills & Boon Reader Service, P.O. Box 236, Croydon, Surrey, CR9 3RU and quote your Subscriber No:...(If applicable) and complete the name and address details below. Alternatively, these books are available from many local Newsagents including W.H.Smith, J.Menzies, Martins and other paperback stockists from 6th July 1992.

Name:..

Address:...

....Post Code:.........................

To Retailer: If you would like to stock M&B books please contact your regular book/magazine wholesaler for details.

You may be mailed with offers from other reputable companies as a result of this application. If you would rather not take advantage of these opportunities please tick box ☐

The truth often hurts . . .

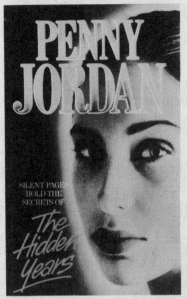

Sometimes it heals

Critically injured in a car accident, Liz Danvers insists her family read the secret diaries she has kept for years – revealing a lifetime of courage, sacrifice and a great love. Liz knew the truth would be painful for her daughter Sage to face, as the diaries would finally explain the agonising choices that have so embittered her most cherished child.

Available now priced £4.99

W**●**RLDWIDE

4 FREE

Romances
and 2 FREE gifts
just for you!

You can enjoy all the
heartwarming emotion of true love for FREE!
Discover the heartbreak and the happiness, the emotion and
the tenderness of the modern relationships in
Mills & Boon Romances.

We'll send you 4 captivating Romances as a special offer from
Mills & Boon Reader Service, along with the chance to have
6 Romances delivered to your door each month.

Claim your FREE books and gifts overleaf...

An irresistible offer from Mills & Boon

Here's a personal invitation from Mills & Boon Reader Service, to become a regular reader of Romances. To welcome you, we'd like you to have 4 books, a CUDDLY TEDDY and a special MYSTERY GIFT absolutely FREE.

Then you could look forward each month to receiving 6 brand new Romances, delivered to your door, postage and packing free! Plus our free Newsletter featuring author news, competitions, special offers and much more.

This invitation comes with no strings attached. You may cancel or suspend your subscription at any time, and still keep your free books and gifts.

It's so easy. Send no money now. Simply fill in the coupon below and post it to -
Reader Service, FREEPOST, PO Box 236, Croydon, Surrey CR9 9EL.

- - - - - - - - - - - - - - **NO STAMP REQUIRED** - - - - - - - - - - - -

Free Books Coupon

Yes! Please rush me 4 free Romances and 2 free gifts! Please also reserve me a Reader Service subscription. If I decide to subscribe I can look forward to receiving 6 brand new Romances each month for just £10.20, postage and packing free. If I choose not to subscribe I shall write to you within 10 days - I can keep the books and gifts whatever I decide. I may cancel or suspend my subscription at any time. I am over 18 years of age.

Ms/Mrs/Miss/Mr _____ EP31R

Address _____

_____

Postcode _____ Signature _____

Offer expires 31st May 1993. The right is reserved to refuse an application and change the terms of this offer. Readers overseas and in Eire please send for details. Southern Africa write to Book Services International Ltd, P.O. Box 42654, Craighall, Transvaal 2024. You may be mailed with offers from other reputable companies as a result of this application.
If you would prefer not to share in this opportunity, please tick box ☐